"[A] subtle and haunting debut . . . From the guilt of a widowed kibbutz dweller in 'On the Border' to Mary McIntyre of 'By the Sea, By the Sea,' whose 'slightly twisted spine' just might explain everything about her, the tales are united in their emphasis on loss and deterioration. An intense, accomplished first collection."

—*Publishers Weekly*

"Swan has a strong command of metaphorical language; to read through this collection is to peruse an old photo album steeped in memory and surprisingly visceral detail. . . . The best of Swan's stories, like 'The Deep,' 'By the Sea, By the Sea,' and 'Max—1970,' are dense prisms reflecting the spectrum of human emotion. . . . The past is 'the deep' plumbed by the most memorable of Swan's characters, and that is where the reader is carried."

—*Library Journal*

"This graceful collection of short stories manages to be both quiet and powerful. The title story interweaves a variety of voices to slowly unravel a mesmerizing tale of twin sisters caught up in each other and World War I. . . . Although several of the stories are set in particular time periods and places, they are all at heart about human relationships and frequently the things people do not say to each other. This allows the stories to be both specific and universal. Even when writing about war, Swan has a calm, almost resigned voice."

—*Booklist*

MARY SWAN is the winner of the 2001 O. Henry Award for short fiction and has been published in several Canadian literary magazines, including *The Malahat Review* and *Best Canadian Stories,* as well as American publications such as *Ontario Review* and Norton's *Sudden Fiction Cont'd.* She lives with her husband and daughter near Toronto, where she works in the library at the University of Guelph.

THE DEEP

AND OTHER STORIES

THE DEEP

AND OTHER STORIES

MARY SWAN

RANDOM HOUSE TRADE PAPERBACKS

NEW YORK

2004 Random House Trade Paperback Edition

This work was originally published in hardcover by Random House, an imprint of
The Random House Publishing Group, a division of Random House, Inc., in 2003.

Some of the stories in this work were originally published in the following
journals and books: *Antigonish Review, Carousel, Malahat Review, Ontario Review,
Coming Attractions* (Oberon, 1999), *O. Henry Prize Stories 2001,*
and *Best Canadian Stories 92* (Oberon, 1992).

LIBRARY OF CONGRESS CATALOGING-IN-PUBLICATION DATA
Swan, Mary
The deep and other stories / Mary Swan.
p. cm.
ISBN 0-8129-6650-3
I. Title.
PR9199.4.S93 D44   2003   813'.6—dc21   2002068099

Printed in the United States of America
Random House website address: www.atrandom.com
2 4 6 8 9 7 5 3 1

Book design by J. K. Lambert

FOR
MY PARENTS,
AND FOR
ALEX AND EMMA

ACKNOWLEDGMENTS

Heartfelt thanks to my editor, Kate Medina,

and my agent, Virginia Barber.

And to Jessica and Elyse for all their help.

CONTENTS

THE DEEP

AND OTHER STORIES

THE DEEP

~~~~~~

AFTER

Here there are two tall windows, very tall, many-paned, and the gauzy white curtains swirl in the breeze, lift and fall like a breath, like a sigh. There is a faint, sweet smell, like blossoms; perhaps it is spring. The leaves on the trees also lift and sigh, all that can be seen through those windows. Sounds reach us from the street, wheels turning and hard shoes and sometimes a voice raised, calling out something, but they are muffled, all these sounds. Distant. Father told us once about the queen's funeral, straw laid in the street to mute the sound. It is like that, and we wonder if someone has died.

HOW TO BEGIN

Has it ever happened to you, that you have wakened suddenly from a long, deep sleep, that it takes some time for you to realize who you are, where you are? Familiar objects, even faces, become mysterious, remote. You stumble about, trailing the fog of sleep into the waking world, and nothing makes sense. Just a few fuddled moments, if you're lucky. Until you splash your face with cold water and recognize it again in the mirror above the basin. Until you drink a cup of tea, breathe fresh air, let routine tasks draw you back. Where do we go, in such a sleep, what is the world that we enter?

It may be France, in 1918.

SURVIVAL SUIT

How to explain it, what it was like? The interview, and then the notice that we were accepted, the official look of it, and then the date for sailing, ten days on. A sudden twinge of panic, of dismay—ten days, such an imaginable length of time. So many things to do, to gather together, the momentum of that carried us for a while. The vaccinations and the endless lists. Blankets and heavy stockings and high boots. Coats, Thermos bottles, sewing case, flannel nightgowns. Knife. Two closely written pages listing essential equipment, with a note at the bottom reminding us that it was our patriotic duty to bring as little luggage as possible.

We laughed about that when we went to dine with Miss Reilly, and she told us how envious she was, how she wished she were setting off too. We talked about the brave boys who had given their lives, James, and the friends and brothers of people we knew. And we reminisced about our European journey, spoke of the spirit of France, of Belgium, of how much we had learned. That time we stood in the little church of San Maurizio, tears streaming down our faces, and how no one thought it strange. Miss Reilly gave us each a slim black pen that evening when we left, so we would remember to write her everything.

The next day Father took us to lunch. Someone had told him that the crossing was more dangerous than anything we'd be close to in France, so after we had eaten, he insisted on going with us to try on lifesaving suits. We saw the flicker in his eyes when the woman said that one suit could support fourteen additional people hanging on to it. But then it was gone, and he said very firmly that we would require two suits. To make him happy, we tried them on all afternoon, though it all seemed quite ridiculous. The heavy rubber suits lined with cork, the snapping steel clamps at chest and ankle, the headgear to buckle on. The woman showed us the special pockets, designed to hold bread and a flask of whiskey, and assured us that along with the fourteen hangers-on, the suit would support the person wearing it for forty-eight hours in a standing position, submerged to just above the waist. "Ophelia!" we said together when we heard this, remembering the doll we had once. The flowers we braided in her long stiff hair and how we tried to float her in the shallow stream. How she kept bobbing up to stand, petals falling everywhere, until we finally tied our heavy wet stockings around her neck and then she did float, but facedown. The trouble from Nan when she found us, not because of the stockings but because we'd been at the stream, and she hadn't known.

We left the store with two bulky parcels, and Father seemed quite relieved that he had been able to purchase what was required to keep us safe.

THE CASTLE

Our mother was a sad woman lying on a couch, on a bed, or very occasionally wrapped in shawls and blankets in a chair on the veranda. We killed her, of course; everyone knew that.

We saw her every day, almost every day, though sometimes only a glimpse from the doorway. Her hazy face, eyes, amid the pillows in the darkened room. Nan holding our hands tightly, keeping us back. Our mother's pale face shifting, swimming toward us through the gloom as she whispered, "Hello, my darlings."

"Hello, my darlings," we mocked sometimes, laughing ourselves silly as we rolled in the soft grass, collecting stains that Nan would scold us for. And we whispered it at night, lying in our narrow beds, holding hands across the gulf between us. *Good night, my darling. Good night, my darling.*

Our mother had a smell, something flowery over something heavier, a little sweet. We recognized it in France, or something very like it. The smell of fear, of despair, of things slowly rotting.

Our brothers said that she had been beautiful. Tall, with shining dark hair that she sometimes wore unpinned, and long silk dresses the color of every flower in the garden. When they came home from school every few months, they spent hours in her room, talking or reading to her; we heard their voices going on and on, with pauses where we imagined her own slipping in. They were much older than we were, with down already forming on their upper lips, and it seemed a different world they described. Picnics and music and parties with candlelight, a cake shaped like a Swiss mountain and mounds of strawberries. These things they told us when we were older. When we were very small they despised us, could not be left alone with us, Nan said, for fear of what might happen.

Once we performed for our mother, turning somersaults all over the front lawn. As we spun and rolled, we heard a sound we didn't recognize; we stood, finally, looking up at the veranda, panting and brushing the hair out of our eyes. In her chair, from the midst of her blankets and shawls, our mother was laughing. She laughed until she cried, until she could hardly catch her breath, and then we stood, resting our heads near her lap, and she stroked our hair and said, "Oh, my dears, it wasn't meant to be this way."

So we understood that we were all under a spell. Crawling through the tangled vines in the kitchen garden we imagined them growing and growing, twining around the big stone house, blotting out the sun, growing thick and fast over the windows of the room where the princess lay sleeping for a hundred years. Smithson roared when we started to hack our way through, so we became more cautious, sitting in a sunny corner popping pods of stolen peas and imagining the prince, the white horse he would ride. How he would sweep Smithson aside and slash his way through the jungle with his sharp sword and ride through the big front door, up the curving stairs, leave his horse grazing in the hallway while he rescued the sleeping princess. Then there would be a feast with a thousand candles blazing; she would wear a sea-green gown shot with silver, and laugh and dance with the prince until morning.

The prince had blue eyes and long fair hair. Years later we found a photograph of our father as a very young man: the face was exactly what we had imagined and we were amazed, for we would never have cast our father as the prince. Or would we? Had we perhaps been shown that picture before, and if so, what did that mean? We talked about it for hours, warming our toes before the stove while a dark rain slashed at the windows, but we reached no conclusion.

Our father also had a smell. He brought it with him from the city, cigars and dust and ashes. As children we grew prickly in his presence, longing to hurl things about, to stick out our tongues, to do something shocking. But terrified too, of saying the wrong thing.

We saw him in his study, usually, before we went to bed. The shadowed room, his face lit strangely from the lamp on the desk, the piles of papers and folders and a thin curl of cigar smoke. We assumed that he blamed us too, and wished we had never been. He asked us if we had been good, if we had done all our lessons, and of course we said yes. Then he called us to him, we walked around the sides of the desk, and he circled his arms about our shoulders, planted kisses on our foreheads, first one, then the other, the scratchy tickle of his mustache. He never called us by our names, and we never tried to fool him as we did everyone else. It would have been pointless, for we were sure he didn't know or care which was which.

When we talked about it later, those nights when the guns went on and on, we wondered if it was just that he didn't know quite what to do with us. He had no sister, no other daughters; he may have been simply ill at ease. And busy, of course. Certainly when we were older, he would talk to us, ask us what we were reading or studying. He seemed to know things that, looking back through a rainy night, suggested he watched us, thought about us. If our mother had been there, perhaps—but then that was the whole point.

THE CORPORAL REMEMBERS

They made me think of horses—well, they would, wouldn't they? Skittish white horses, dream horses, maybe. You know how they raise their hooves, their legs, holding them in the air, trying so hard to become weightless, not touch the ground. I can't explain. But that's what they made me think of. That's all.

THE FOUNTAIN

There is a portrait of our mother; it hangs in our father's study, a dark room even on the brightest of days. The artist stayed in our house while he worked on it, and Nan still talks with some surprise about how he made her laugh. And there is another picture, painted at the same time. A quick, light sketch in soft colors that used to hang by the fire, until our father let Marcus take it away to his own house.

In this second picture our mother wears a soft yellow dress and sits on the edge of a fountain. James and Marcus are two young boys in shades of blue, sitting on either side, all of them looking down at something she holds in her lap. From the position, the shape of her mouth, her half-parted lips, it looks as if she is reading them a story, though it seems a strange place to do that. We used to love that picture when we were young, used to stare and stare at it. The grass so exactly the color of rich, late spring grass, and the way he painted the spray from the fountain, a glistening in the air. It hung on the wall by the fire like a window to another world, and it seemed quite possible that by staring hard enough, we could step right through.

There is a signature in the bottom corner of the painting, and a date. When we were older we realized from the date that we were already growing beneath the yellow dress, getting ready to smash that world to pieces.

The fountain doesn't exist any longer; the space where it stood holds a circular bed of flowers that change with the seasons. We caused that too. When we were small, two at the most, the silly girl who helped care for us fell asleep beneath a shady tree. We don't remember her; they say we can't remember any of it, we were far too young. But we do remember, we are certain we do. The prismed spray of the fountain, the sound and feel of it. Like the feeling, not just the thought, of being hand in hand. The way the water was neither hot nor cold but exactly the temperature to welcome us in. It wasn't deep, but we were very small, and it was deep enough to close over our heads. And we remember the magic of underwater, the absolute silence and peace. It's not likely there were fish in that fountain, but we remember the color, darting streaks of light.

Somehow we must have pulled each other out, though when we think of how it was inside, we wonder why. We must have clambered back over the side and begun to walk, walking ahead of our wet footprints, toward the big house where a door was already opening, a white shape running. Walking hand in hand toward everything that came after.

This happened on a bright day in June. We know that; we've been told. So why do we have another picture in our minds, every bit as clear? The grass brown and dead, trees bare except for a few withered curls of leaf that rattle when the wind comes. Two people, large and dark, with dark heavy feet, carry two small bodies, held forward in their arms like an offering about to be deposited on a stone. Water drips from the sky, and from the sodden bundles, and there is a vast silence.

MRS. MOORE

They were angels. And by that I don't just mean they were good, although they were that. Kind and hardworking, generous with their time and money. Not minding what they did. I had my doubts when I first met them. Even bedraggled as they were from the journey, they clearly hadn't done a hard day's work in their lives. We'd had a few like that—not many, but a few who couldn't take it. Who had some vision of themselves passing plates of cucumber sandwiches or wheeling some handsome boy about the garden. Garden! And there were some who were there for a good time—well, why not, I said. As long as they did their work, as long as they were there when I needed them, what business of mine was it?

Listen to me now: I would have shocked myself speechless a few years ago. But those poor boys, the look in their eyes and their poor broken bodies, the way they twitched and jumped but were always ready with a joke, with a smile. And some of the women—well, they wouldn't have much of a chance, would they, otherwise, if I tell the truth. Which makes you wonder, doesn't it, what it takes for a fellow to overlook thick ankles, a crossed eye. Like I said, as long as I could count on them to be where they should, to do their work, as long as they didn't get themselves diseased or worse and become a problem—who am I to say they shouldn't take some pleasure while they could?

Not that the twins were like that, nothing like. If anything, they were a bit too much the other way. Too serious, you know, and I don't think they'd had much to do with men in their lives. Not romantically, I mean. There was a young fellow they went around with for a while. I don't know what was in it, only friendly, I would imagine. My friend Dr. Thomas told me the boy was having a course of treatment—you know. Like so many. Although usually it was the French girls to blame for that, and this boy didn't look— well, he didn't look like he'd ever be wanting for companionship, if you know what I mean. He looked like he could be choosy.

Though the way things were over there, I suppose that's no guarantee. Not if half the things my friend the colonel says are true.

So this boy—I can't think of his name right now, but he was a devil all right. And such a joker; he had a gift for that. No matter what kind of mood you were in when you ran into him, you'd be laughing by the time he moved on. He wasn't in our camp too long, a couple of weeks, maybe. Though he'd pop up every once in a while after, to see the twins. And that charm of his worked on them too, you could tell. They were lighter, somehow, when he was around. Like I say, though, I don't know what was in it. I'd never known any twins, not really, until I met Esther and Ruth. They were like you'd imagine twins to be, if you had to imagine. Same voice, same expressions, moved the same way. And always *we*—I'd forgotten that, I guess I got so used to it. We did this, we think that, never *I*. After a time they started wearing different-colored ribbons around their wrists, so people could tell them apart, but I always had the feeling they used to switch those around, like some private joke. Or maybe it didn't matter to them. I used to wonder sometimes. I mean, it's bad enough if two friends fall for the same young man, especially if he's a bit of a scoundrel like that one. It seems I heard he was wounded at the end of the war, or had some trouble, but I don't remember what it was. Ah well, it's all water under the bridge—oh Lordy, I didn't mean to say that.

THE HEADMISTRESS — I

There will be those who think it is somehow my fault. Not say it, perhaps, but think it. Their father may. He came to see me in my office, sat in the green chair, refused a cup of tea. Asked me to persuade them not to go, and never to tell them that he had asked.

"You have influence," he said. "They would listen to you, to what you say."

At the time I told him I had no right to do that. Told him they were grown women, twenty-six years old, they had to make their own decisions. I pretended, and I see now that it was pretending, that I didn't know what he meant by *influence*. As if I'd never said any of the things I've said, lived the life I've lived. He recognized the pretense; that showed behind his gold spectacles. But all he said was "Very well." And we talked of general things until he left. We have always just missed saying things to each other, their father and I.

It is cold out tonight, and a vicious sleet smashes against the window. But I sit here by the fire, quite warm and dry, a tray close at hand, my books, my pen. It comes to me that all the things I've said and done, all the battles fought, have been from this position of warmth and comfort. This morning at the school I looked down on those rows of upturned faces and thought that they receive my message from the same position of comfort. No fault of theirs, but what about mine?

I believed I was sending them into the world well equipped, year after year, a generation of women proud of their minds, secure in their worth, who believed in truth, in beauty, who would spread that belief by their very existence. I believed that the world would have to become a better place, that they would see to that. Perhaps I should have given them armor. Taught them to think but not to feel, taught them to save themselves. I say this in all seriousness.

I have said that we always seemed to just miss saying things, their father and I. Now I have to stop and think about that. I met him first almost fifteen years ago; I have known him longer than I knew my own parents. We were interviewing each other, I suppose, about the possibility of the girls attending the school. I had been to a meeting outside and was taking the tram back through an unfamiliar part of the city. I remember that I was a little worried about being late, that I was in that state of heightened awareness that comes when your surroundings are strange, when you must actually use your eyes and ears. The streets, the houses we skimmed by were like those I knew, and yet not. The people getting on and off like that too. As if a glass had shifted to distort, ever so slightly. Like those moments in a dream when little things are odd enough to make you wonder if you *are* dreaming. It was summer, the trees in full dark leaf, and a steady rain fell from a sky that was a vast, washed gray. The tram was a cocoon moving through it, and the people who pulled themselves on from outside were giddy with the rain, but gently so. Some soaked to the skin, wiping water from their hands and cheeks. A middle-aged woman scattering droplets from her black umbrella as she closed it, laughing as she caught her breath and saying things to herself that would have had us looking carefully away at any other time or place. But it was clear, there, that it was rain madness, nothing more. We were all touched with it.

That was what I came from the day I met their father. Still worried about the time, I remember hurrying down the corridor to my new office, lighting the lamps, sending for tea. I was expecting the tea when the soft tap at the door came, and I was quite taken aback when a gray-haired man walked into my room. He looked like what he was, a successful man of business, yet there was something hesitant about the way he crossed the threshold, something that made me immediately want to put him at ease. I remember that he told me right away that his wife was dead. I knew, of course, and knew she had been for a number of years, and I thought it strange he would mention it like that. But then I remembered who he was, his reputation in the world of business, and realized it was probably deliberate, some kind of tactic. First words, after all, can be as calculated as the clothing we put on, the faces we compose to meet someone or to face the world.

Mr. A. went on to tell me his sons had gone away to school from the beginning, but he had always wished to keep his daughters, then eleven, at home. From all he had found out, he said, it seemed my school would provide the type of education he wished them to have, with the added advantage of being only a short train ride from their home, so they could attend as day pupils. "They're clever girls," he said, "but a little—"

There was another tap at the door, really the tea this time, and we fussed about with cups and tiny spoons. He drank his clear, as I usually do, but for some reason that day I added milk and sugar. The lights pushed the rain-colored air to the corners of the room, and I remember thinking that it was another cocoon, like the tram. This circle of light where we sat, the music of silver spoons.

"They don't really know other children," he said, after lifting his cup to his lips. "We live a very quiet life where we are. And they seem quite content, but I've been thinking . . . Also, they are growing up, you see . . ."

"Of course," I said, and then he said, "I was born a twin myself, but my brother didn't survive," and while I was wondering what to say to that, he took off his glasses and rubbed at his left eye, saying, "How strange, I don't think I've ever told anyone that."

I didn't believe him, thinking it was another part of some peculiar strategy. The same way he showed his face, vulnerable without the spectacles.

As it happened, at that particular time we were rather desperate for new pupils, but I had learned a few tricks myself. I suggested that he come back with the girls, bringing a sample of their current work. I told him that although we usually had a long waiting list, there was a possibility we could accept them both for the fall term.

How much of it is my fault? Or because of my influence, which comes to the same thing. Those letters they wrote, my responses. Before they stopped writing. You see, I thought what they needed was reassurance. That they were doing the right thing, that it was all worthwhile. And I believed it was, it's not that I lied. But reading their letters again, I can't believe I was so blind; my whole being cringes when I think of the letters I wrote back.

Am I too hard on myself? It's true that only now, after so many have returned, telling their stories, now that we see who has become rich, or richer, what the world is still like, only now is it all so clear. But I failed them, there's no escaping that. What they told me was not what I myself believed, and instead of listening I tried to nudge them back to my way. So much for all those fine words about confidence and identity. I failed them, and now they're dead.

Many years ago I knew a young man who died of a fever in Africa. If I had agreed to marry him, he would not have gone to Africa, would not have caught the fever, would not have died. But I did not agree, because I was already taking the first steps along what I believed was my proper path. Because in marrying him I believed that I would have lost control of my life, and even though I still believe that would have been true, I am no longer so certain it would have been the worst thing. After the death of my parents, I was raised by an aunt and uncle. They were ignorant people; things happened in their house that I have not told a soul. My parents had left some money for my education, and I understood this would be my means of escape, my way of saving myself. I know that I didn't kill him, that earnest young man whose face I can no longer recall. A fever killed him. But it can't be denied that I played a part. As with Ruth and Esther. I remember that first day when their father took off his glasses and rubbed at his eye, and I realize suddenly that I could talk to him about this, that he is perhaps the only person I could talk to about this. Except for the fact that he is the last person in the world I could talk to about this.

SAILING

We stood at the railing, looking down at the mass of people, and just as we spotted our father he took off his hat and waved it frantically in the air. We had never known him to do such a thing. We were too far away to see anything more than the dark overcoat, the pale blob that was his face, his hand clutching the waving black hat. But we were struck by an astonishing thought. It was as if we were really seeing him. Over that distance, in the midst of all the noise and confusion, we saw something completely unexpected. Our father always moved slowly, deliberately, and we realized that we pictured him motionless, like a photograph. Sitting at his desk in a pool of light, or at the dinner table. Even at the wheel of his new motor car, he was somehow still while the machine hurtled through space. We remembered how he ran up the stairs the day our mother died, how we had no idea he could move so fast. The very air, after he had rushed past, was shivering and charged. The same thing now in the frenzied waving of his hat. As if something had burst from him, alone in the crowd on the dock.

A girl stood beside us at the rail, a girl with very blue eyes and light-colored hair tucked under a funny little hat, made from the same material as her coat. When our eyes met, she gave a small smile and said, "I don't know why I'm looking down, there's no one here to say good-bye." Then she turned and walked quickly away, leaving us wondering whether we should follow. But then the ship began to move, and we watched the land fall away, imagining, long after it was possible, that we still saw the black speck of our father's waving hat.

We told ourselves that it was no different from any other crossing. There were uniforms, and a disproportionate number of young people on board, but we had been to Europe twice before. It was not, we said, as if we were going into something completely unfamiliar. What can have been in our minds?

The girl's name was Elizabeth. We shared a table with her at dinner that first night, and came to know her well on the voyage. It was not difficult to know her well; we had never met a person who talked so freely, so openly. We learned very quickly that she was going overseas to find her brother. Arthur, his name was. Art. He was nineteen, a little more than two years younger than she was, and he had gone over as an ambulance driver just after his eighteenth birthday. Her family hadn't heard from him in five or six months, and their mother was terribly worried. And she had enough to worry about without that, poor Mother, with Elizabeth's father being so sick and four younger ones at home, such a tiny bit of money to live on. So they held a family meeting one night in the kitchen and decided that Elizabeth should volunteer, so she could be over there and find out where he was, how he was. Their mother was tormented by the thought that he was in a hospital somewhere, alone and suffering, missing them. The other possibility she didn't allow anyone to mention.

Elizabeth had already taken a nursing course; she got interested when her father became ill, so she was accepted without any problem. Someone had told her not to mention Art when she went to be interviewed, so she didn't, although she felt terrible keeping it back. Somehow her mother found the money to get most of the things Elizabeth needed to take, and made her a new coat and hat out of an overcoat that her father wouldn't wear again. But there was no money left over for anyone to travel with her to the city, so they had to say good-bye at the station, and she missed them all so; she'd never spent a night away from home before.

We pictured it as Elizabeth talked, pictured it as a scene from a sentimental novel, so removed from our own experience. The scrubbed table in the warm kitchen, the dishes cleared away, the kettle simmering on the stovetop. All of them there except Father, whose coughing could be heard from upstairs. Mother looking so tired, her hands swollen and chapped. Young Bob, who was trying desperately to grow a mustache. He thought he should be the one to go, thought he could lie about his age, but Mother said absolutely not, and besides, she needed him at home. Bob was fourteen and growing almost as quickly as he thought he was. Nessie thought she should go too, so Elizabeth wouldn't be all alone, but they needed the money she brought in, and she didn't have the nursing course, so they didn't think she'd have much luck trying to go by herself. Peter and Amy were too young, but they were there, Amy sitting on her red cushion, watching and listening. When it was decided, Elizabeth and her mother went upstairs to tell Father, but he fell asleep before they'd finished.

We didn't tell Elizabeth much about our own family, talking instead about things we'd heard about the war, about our European journeys, about France the last time we saw it. About red-roofed villages and the quiet of the countryside, small cobbled squares. The food in Paris, the gardens and museums and galleries. We told all this to Elizabeth, who cheerfully said that she didn't know a thing about art, but perhaps she'd have a chance to learn. What else could we have told her that would not have seemed grotesque? That we'd heard our mother laugh once? That our father bought us rubber suits and waved his hat as we sailed away? That our brother Marcus didn't see us off, not because he couldn't afford to but because he had a business luncheon? We couldn't tell her about James for obvious reasons, but even if we had, she couldn't have understood how it was. Perhaps it was because our brothers were so much older, because they went away to school, because they were cruel to us when we were young. Perhaps that was why they didn't seem connected to us, like the most casual of acquaintances. When we heard that James had been killed we were sad, but in a strangely abstract way. Like hearing about the brother of someone you went to school with or met at a dance. It was different for Marcus, of course, and for our father. The light burning in his study until morning, a smell of whiskey on occasion.

After James enlisted he came home to collect some things, and we were alone in the house one afternoon. Rain fell outside the tall windows and the rooms were chill; we had a fire lit and sat reading beside it. James came in, restless, pacing about the room. Touching pictures, the vase on the mantel, a dish on the table. He was a little stocky, James, his oiled hair thinning already, his chin square and his eyes pale. We saw that he would look very like our father, when he reached his age.

Finally James stopped pacing and drew another chair closer to the fire, sat drumming the fingers of his right hand on his knee. We closed our books and asked him something—when he would sail, likely, or if he had everything he needed. He answered, and then began to talk about others he knew who were going at the same time or had already sailed. How he couldn't wait to be there in the thick of it, whipping the Hun, all those phrases that came so easily to everyone's lips in those days. "Poor Marcus," he said. "He'll miss all the fun."

And then, being James, he went on and on about what a lot of fools the generals were, how they were doing it all wrong, how what was needed was—well, we didn't really listen, we'd heard it before. He got up to put another log on the fire and burned his finger arranging it. We looked up at his exclamation and saw him put his finger in his mouth, and we noticed at the same instant that his eyes were glistening in the firelight, that there were tears in his pale eyes. And one of us said, "Are you afraid, James?" It was a moment to ask and be answered, and he took his finger from his mouth, looked at it, and said, "Oh yes."

That was all. The next minute he strode over to draw the heavy curtains against the fading day, then left the room. Back to camp, onto a ship, then marching down a dark, rutted road on the way to the trenches for the first time. The scream of a shell, and nothing more.

We tell ourselves that it is too easy to call a moment by a crackling fire the true moment. To say that the glint of tears was more real than the childhood cruelty, the adult arrogance and bluster. Our brother James was not particularly likable, meant little to us, nor we to him. Our sadness when he died was more because that was so. A moment in a rainy room just one of the things we remember, should we happen to think of him. We knew that this would have been incomprehensible to Elizabeth, perhaps appalling.

But is it true, what we've said about James? What we felt, what we didn't feel? Is it possible that it was really like that, all our life before? So removed. Or does it merely seem so from here? Here where things are so different, where what we think about is the cocoa, will it hold out? And where can we get some eggs. How much our feet hurt, the long soak we will give them if we can get hot water. Will our headache ever go, can we stand it another hour, two, the noise and the heat and the pounding. Will this one ever come back, or that one.

Walking back to the hut one gray afternoon, boards over mud that was almost frozen and so quiet, suddenly, the canteen left behind. The sky heavy, air cold and dense with the rain that had fallen, would fall again. By the tree we called the last tree in Europe, Hugh sat writing. He had a wooden chair he'd scrounged somewhere, a couple of boards laid over some empty tins. He was wearing a gray sweater the color of dense smoke, pearled with moisture from the air, holes in one elbow. Black pipe clenched between his teeth, smoke, more gray, wisping up. We were on our way to sleep, thinking of nothing but the chill in our bones, how wonderful it was to walk through such silence to a damp cot, to wrap the blankets tight, close our eyes. We were happy with that, wanted nothing more from life, and the sight of Hugh in his smoke-colored sweater became all entwined with that moment of perfect contentment.

THE HEADMISTRESS—II

Mr. A. brought the girls to meet me a week later. I was sleeping better by then; the day was sunny and warm and I felt calm and quite like myself, none of the eeriness surrounding our first meeting. It's difficult—I came to know them well over many years, or thought I did, so it's difficult to look back to that first meeting, clear of any of the knowledge or familiarity that came later. What struck me first, I think, was their calmness. They were not especially beautiful children, but there was something very appealing about them. Their long hair was tied back neatly, and though they weren't dressed identically, they somehow gave that impression. When they were not responding to one of my questions, they both looked down at their polished shoes, the toes just brushing the floor. This did not seem like shyness or deference. Rather it was as if they returned to some serious and self-contained contemplation. They replied politely to anything I asked, and whichever one answered spoke in the plural. I'd forgotten that, but I remember how it struck me at the time, the way they never spoke together. But there was no hesitation, no collision, conversation flowing easily from one or the other so that the effect was of talking to a single person.

It's an interesting exercise, this recollection, the way it makes you remember more and more. Like opening a door, having no control over who walks through. Since I heard the news, I've been looking at photographs. Ones from that European trip, several that they sent me from Paris, in their uniforms. But it wasn't until after the memorial service that I made myself bring out the oldest. I suppose it was seeing everyone there, all the old pupils. A year or two after they came to the school we received an unexpected bequest, and decided to use part of it to make a proper photographic record of the rooms, of the teachers and pupils. At the end of the year I gave each one a small individual portrait in a leather folder.

The photographer we hired was a talented young man several years younger than myself. Jones, his name was, and he had a soft Welsh voice to go with it. He went west later, and I don't know what happened to him. But we had several lengthy conversations about art, about photography and painting. I would have thought, if I had thought about it at all, that photography was a scientific process, a way of recording reality; would have thought that was the marvel of it. But Mr. Jones made me see it differently. He said, for example, that while a painter has all kinds of tricks at his disposal— different materials, different brushes and brush strokes, all the colors of the rainbow—a photographer works only with light and shadow. This particular conversation took place in an empty classroom. There was a wild blue sky through the tall windows, the tops of flame-colored trees.

"This moment," Mr. Jones said, "were I to photograph it, the record of reality would be a man and a woman talking in an empty room. Now, if I were a painter, I could add things. The color of that sky, the leaves, and I could pick up that color at the throat of your dress, perhaps a touch on your cheekbones. I could change your expression slightly, or my own, the curve of your lips, and the painting would not be about an empty room.

"But what can I do?" he went on. "What can I do with my

camera? Oh, there are some tricks. Those photographs for your booklet—there are ways to make rooms look bigger, the view more enticing. But how do I photograph a moment, this moment, say, and have it clear that the leaves outside the window are not the soft green of spring, that the year is dying and not beginning? I must pull out the truth of it, of a person or a place. If there is to be anything real, I must draw out the heart."

I don't remember what happened next, but there was truth in what he said, and the photographs are the proof. I have them all together in a folder, a record of a particular year of my life.

Mr. Jones spent a great deal of time in the school that autumn. He was clearly an artist and not a businessman, for he was paid one price to provide photographs of each teacher and pupil, yet he took some again and again until he was satisfied, going away with the plates and coming back to try once more. In his studio he showed me the different attempts, laying them out on a round table covered with a rich blue cloth, and I understood what he meant.

Of course, he had more tricks than he admitted. I observed all the individual sittings; it would not have been proper otherwise, even in 1905. I saw the way he arranged the light or the folds of a dress, positioned the arms. The way the sitter submitted totally, becoming somehow inanimate while he moved limbs, smoothed the hair, turned the chin just a fraction. Called for different props—a book, a flute, a flower. But the end result, trick or not, was as he had said. Some essence of the women and girls I knew captured in a way that was quite astounding. In the end it was only the twins who gave him trouble. He came back for them repeatedly, all through that cold, dark December, until finally he admitted defeat and posed them together.

My own photograph both pleases and disturbs me. I remember every sitting vividly, at the school and in his studio, yet I can't imagine a moment when I looked like this. I know I faced the camera straight on, unafraid, yet my eyes somehow slide off, away from it. My hair is dressed as I have always worn it, yet it seems to be struggling to escape. Wisps have worked free to dance along my cheek, to wave in the soft light about my head. My hands are folded as I remember, but there is a tension in the fingers, and the bottom hand is slightly blurred, as if caught in a sudden movement. And I am certain my mouth has never looked like this. The photograph pleases me, as a work of art might; it invites one to understand certain things about the woman in it. But I have never recognized it as myself.

LETTER

Dear Father,

Thank you so much for your latest package, which arrived safely two days ago. We are greedily devouring the books and chocolate, and the stockings are a godsend. Please thank Janet—we assume she bought them—and tell her how glad we are to get them, as what we brought is much bedarned. We were very sorry to hear about John Tupper.

You ask where we are—we can't say exactly, though we can tell you that we are fairly close to the front, but not in any danger. This is a sort of interim camp for men on their way to or from the front. Sometimes they go from here to a real rest camp, sometimes right back up to the line. When we first came here, we stayed in a tent pitched on the stubble field behind the camp. Very damp and cold. Just last week we moved into a room made from an old storeroom at the end of the canteen hut. Small, but it seems like a palace to us after the tent. We have just enough room for two cots with their now-dry straw mattresses and our trunks, and one of the boys pounded some nails into the walls so we can hang up our tin hats, gas masks, and clothes. We also have a little stove but don't need to use it much now that the nights are not so cold. The hills round about are covered with wildflowers this time of year, and in our free time, if we are not sleeping—which we seem to do a great deal of— we have lovely long walks.

As you see, we are well settled in and the routine of our days no longer seems at all strange. We generally mess with the officers, and the food is plentiful, though not particularly satisfying. Mornings we spend washing hundreds of mugs from the previous night in the canteen, and preparing sandwiches and sometimes cakes and sweets for the afternoon and evening. Two little French boys keep us supplied with wood for the small stove, which is all we have to heat the huge kettles of cocoa and coffee that we go through each day. In addition to ourselves and Mrs. Moore, who is in charge, a woman named Berthe from the nearby village helps out. She speaks no English, and as Mrs. Moore knows no French, we do a great deal of translating and thank heaven for those classes at Miss Reilly's. We had a letter from her last week and she mentioned that she saw you at dinner at the Barretts'. It is so strange sometimes to think of life going on at home just like before. You would be amazed at the life we have settled into here, but settled in we have. The work is hard and might be seen as monotonous, but we know it's important, the boys so appreciative of any little thing we do for them. There are always a few who can barely read or write, and if there's time we often write letters to their dictation. And mend torn shirts or sew on stripes or badges. All kinds of little things that mean a great deal over here. We can't, as we said, tell you where we are, but we are close enough to hear the guns. Don't worry, though, we have been assured that the camp will move if the fighting draws much closer.

There is a large hospital in a beautiful old château a few miles from here, and on our free day we usually go there to do what we can to help out. We read to the soldiers or write more letters, help feed those who need help. The nurses are wonderful but so busy; they are always glad to see us. So you see our days are very full and we really have no time to miss home, so you mustn't worry about that. We must close now as it is very late and we will be rising with the sun.

STAIN

When our mother actually died, you might have thought we would have been prepared for it. Living her half-life for years. Off in her upstairs room the last long time, just a hint of recognition in her sunken eyes, and that only sometimes. You might have thought we would have gotten on with our lives, that she would have been a sad, fixed point outside our orbit. What we would have thought at the time, if we had to explain it. For our father, too, who rarely saw her, as far as we knew, who inquired after her health, her day, when the nurse sat down to eat with us, as one would of a mutual acquaintance.

It was Sunday morning. Early June, that time of year when the sky is blue every time you open your eyes, when the lilac blossoms fill the air. The night nurse was having a cup of tea in the kitchen, talking about carrots and peas, and we were coming through the door, blinking after the light outside, our shoes wet with dew.

Then someone cried out, and we ran too; ahead of us the door of the study flung open, our father with his shirtsleeves caught up, running up the stairs, we'd never seen him move like that. The gold pen falling from his hand to roll and rattle, a small distinct noise amid the calls, the sound of thumping feet. Mrs. B. coming after, stooping to pick it up automatically, not even looking, slipping it into her apron pocket where it continued to ooze. The dark, spreading stain on her apron pocket—it seemed that stain spread out slowly to cover our whole lives.

MARCUS

They were always strange, always trouble. From the very beginning, when they took our mother away. We were called home from school to see her before she died, although as it happened her dying took years. But those days we were home when the house was hushed and strange, we would hear their thin squalling in the night. James thought we should kill them, and we tried a few times. I don't remember how, childish things I'm sure, but someone always stopped us. In the end we were glad to go back to school.

As they grew up they stopped squalling and took to whispering, heads together. The sound of a couple of snakes. They had their own language for a while, a lot of nonsense words that they seemed to understand completely. The day of Mother's funeral they sliced themselves up with broken glass and had to be carried upstairs, screaming and kicking and getting blood everywhere. And how glad James and I were to hear them screaming even louder while Nan and Mrs. B. scrubbed their wounds with alcohol. When Father sent us up to the nursery later, they were sitting in bed with their legs all bandaged, eating cake, looking pale and oh so smug.

THE WAR BOOK

It began to seem, after a time, that everyone had something. One thing they'd seen or heard that they couldn't shake off, that they carried, would carry forever, like a hard, dull stone in the heart. Not obvious things, not blood and mayhem, for that was everywhere and there was nothing exceptional about that. But it might be the shell of a house seen through a train window. A small place in what remained of a village they passed by, part of two walls left standing and a mess of rubble inside. It might lead to an obsessive need to discover—or maybe just to wonder—what was the name of the village, who had lived in that house, what had happened, what *exactly* had happened to them. Or it might be a rope swing still hanging from a blasted tree, the line of a little girl's neck in an echoing black station, one half of a beautiful bowl. A woman in black whacking the backside of a crying child all along a deserted street. Why was the child crying? Not that there weren't reasons enough to cry, but what was it right then? Or a creased photograph found somewhere, no way to know anything about the people in it, not even what side they were on. A white cat sleeping in a patch of sunlight, a piece of music heard in a most unlikely place. We thought if we could gather those things together, we would call it *The War Book*. And that would be the only way to communicate it, to give someone an idea of how it was.

Hugh's story concerned his friend Tom, the one he grew up with, joined up with. They'd stayed together against all the odds, and one frosty morning they were standing on the fire step when Hugh saw something glittering in the frozen mud at his feet. He bent to pick it up; his fingers were numb and he fumbled at it, cursed. "What?" Tom said, turning his head, looking down at the spot where Hugh crouched. And then, with a thud, he was lying with his dead eyes looking *up* at the spot where Hugh crouched with the glittering object between his fingers, and Hugh remembers looking at it, seeing that it was only a jagged bit of wood, something that never could have glittered at all.

So Hugh's story is about mathematics, about physics, about how he tried to work it all out. The chances of the sniper's bullet finding that exact spot at the base of Tom's ear. The distance to the other side, and whether the bullet had already left the gun when Hugh suddenly crouched. He drew diagrams, tried to work out where the other man had been, how tall he was, what he looked like. Did he squeeze the trigger slowly or with a sudden burst of excitement? Hugh called on everything he'd learned in that school a world away, smell of chalk dust in his nostrils, the way it looked, floating in the sunlight through the high windows, the creak of his desk chair, the oiled floor. He knew he hadn't paid enough attention—he'd usually copied Tom's assignments, after all. But he thought he could learn what he needed to know.

And he thought about all the things that could have made a difference. If he hadn't seen the glittering thing that couldn't possibly have glittered, he and Tom would have remained standing as they were, the bullet would have thumped into the wall of the trench behind them, between them, or maybe not come at all. Or the sniper himself—if he'd had to scratch his nose, if someone had called to him, some noise had made him look away for only an instant. If he'd had a cut on his finger, making it a little stiff, if his eyelashes had been longer, his vision slightly blurred.

When that kind of thinking drove Hugh mad, he would think instead about the bullet. The place where it was made—gloomy, he pictured it, and very noisy. Heat and sparks flying. Its long journey even to get to the fingers that loaded it into the gun. All the things that could have changed it even then. The temperature that that morning, so clear and cold with no wind; but what if there had been? Or not even a wind but some tiny shift in the currents of air, the last breath of a storm that whirled around a mountain somewhere, the disturbance of someone running, even a cough. If someone had coughed in Paris—one of us, say, we were there. If one of us had coughed in Paris at exactly the right moment, would Tom still be alive?

RAIN

So tired tonight, too tired to do anything, even to order scattered thoughts. Silent except for the rain that splatters against the window, against the flimsy walls of the hut, splatters fitfully, as if tossed by a bored child. Think of the rain falling here, how it must be falling all over the country, all the way to the coast, to the grim Atlantic. Roiling there, a tumbled picture in black and white, the winds that toss those waves driving the rain on. Only in that deep, wintry zone far beneath is everything still and silent, suspended in dark green light. But up above the rain sweeps on, rolls over another shore. Splatters like this against the windows of our old room, but the room is empty, we are not there. Even if we were to return, it would be empty; quite impossible, now, for us to be there.

IN HIS STUDY THE FATHER
CLOSES HIS EYES

And thinks about what he has lost. It is very quiet, and although his children were never noisy, he knows that this is the silence of their absence, that it will be like this for the rest of his life.

He will sell the house. The big house in the country, bought with the first of his money. The place where the happy life was to be lived. How can it be that they're all gone? Alice. James. Esther and Ruth. His daughters brushed his cheek with their cool lips, first Esther, with the slightly higher arch to her eyebrow, then Ruth. The ship waited, a big, hard lump of the inevitable. He waved like a madman, swept off his hat and waved that too, long after the ship began to move away. Thinking that if he stopped at all he would snap the fragile thread, that they would lose sight of the place they must come back to and gently drift away forever. His shoulder ached for days, and he welcomed it.

Marcus is not gone, Marcus is still alive. In his rooms in the city, surrounded by furniture no longer needed in the big house, by his own things from when he was a boy. The painting of the happy life hangs near Marcus's bed, where the father need never see it. Marcus is still alive, still in the business, still making money. And he might still marry, have children who will run and jump and tumble, the juice of different fruits smeared on their chins.

Could they belong to Marcus, these ghost children who flicker behind the father's eyes? Marcus, the pale second son, the one who was always there, two steps behind James, even when he grew to be the taller. What does Marcus feel, suddenly an only child? They meet in the office or outside it, with sheaves of paper or without, and there is an amazing harmony, the way they think about the business, the way it lives for them, what they see in its future. The war years have been good for them, extremely good, and the father wonders if Marcus also feels guilty at the way he can't help being pleased with that. Excited by that. Distracted from his grief.

Perhaps they do belong to Marcus, the ghost children whose

running footsteps patter along the floors above his head. Perhaps Marcus will meet the right woman and find himself a completely different life. But the father remembers that he himself found the right woman, that it guaranteed nothing but this long night alone in the creaking house.

And there was Anne Reilly, the girls' headmistress. A handsome woman, intelligent and witty. Comfortable with children. She would have looked just right, through candlelight, at the end of the table. In all his encounters with her over the years, there had been this flutter of possibility. But he could never get to it through the thicket of their first meeting. He had been expecting an older woman, although she had been, at the time, older than he'd assumed. When he opened the door she was reaching to secure a hairpin and she completed the movement before she spoke, without any hint of awkwardness. The hem of her dress was damp; he could tell by the way it moved as she came around the desk toward him, saying something about the weather. He wondered what she had been doing out in the rain, and realized that he would have believed anything at all. Posting a letter or riding a white horse or dancing around a pagan altar.

As he settled into a chair, he was astonished to hear himself say, "My wife has died." And it terrified him, the way she had so effortlessly drawn those words from his very heart, words he hadn't even realized were lurking there. He wondered if she was at all aware of this power, and many years later he still wondered. From that point he was always somehow on guard with her, he couldn't help it, for she was someone who could lay you bare in an instant. Just once, when the girls showed him the official letter, when they quietly went about gathering up the things they would need, just then he tried to speak, to enlist her help. She pretended she didn't know what he meant, pretended they were just two people, talking about two other people. He had left as quickly as he could, numbed by another loss.

Later, in the shop, his heart was sick, watching them try things on. The heavy rubber, the ridiculous headgear, and all he could see was the two of them, bobbing alone in the vast gray waste of some ocean.

SOLDIERS — I

Hugh told us this story, about a man named Baker. Known as Silly Sam when he worked as a comedian, before. One day he was blown up; they dug him out quickly, and he seemed to be all right. They were due to be relieved in a few days anyway, and they'd lost so many men that they couldn't spare him, so he stayed in the line. But as it happened, there was a push somewhere, and their relief didn't come for nearly two weeks, and Baker had to be sent back before that, because he started to cry. Slowly at first, a few tears splashing onto his muddy knees where he crouched, trying to eat a chunk of bread. The concussion, they all thought, it does funny things to your body. But it got worse. "This makes no sense," Baker would say, "I'm the happiest man in France!" It stopped when he was sleeping, but they had little time for that, and the minute he opened his eyes the tears began to well up, roll down his cheeks, splash on his tunicfront. So thick and fast he had to wipe his cheeks constantly, and in the end he was so busy doing that he couldn't even hold his rifle. Then they sent him back.

SOLDIERS — II

There was a pig of a man named Smythe. Little eyes, flicking like a snake's. In the canteen, when the cigarettes were gone, the battered cauldrons of cocoa empty. "Let me help you with that," lifting the heavy pot from the fire. Then an arm about the waist, squeezing, his breath foul, stained teeth beneath the mustache and stubbly chin rubbing, and then a voice said, "That's enough," and he was gone, scuttering out the back door. That was how we first met Hugh.

SOLDIERS — III

It was only a trick of the Paris traffic that had us pause behind them. The woman's face turned to look. Nothing in her expression, she was just looking back. It was a staff car, we could see the dark shape of the driver's head. And we thought—for this is how we've changed or learned—maybe she'll get a decent meal out of it, maybe he'll take her somewhere where the cutlery sparkles and nothing is in short supply, the officer belonging to the scratchy-uniformed arm that rested on the seat behind her. Right as we thought that, his large white hand splayed on the back of her head, forcing it down.

And we remembered Neufchâteau, the Hotel Agriculture, in the afternoon. Waiting in that dingy, smoky lobby for someone to get us out of there. Across the street a few tables crowded the narrow sidewalk, and we went there to drink a cup of coffee. Beside us, two soldiers and a boy of ten or eleven. They were giving him tumblers of wine to drink, and chocolate from their pockets. He didn't speak any English, but they kept putting their hands on his shoulders, saying, "Friends, *oui?* Friends."

These men are also dying in the trenches—can it be right to think that less of a tragedy? The cowards, the liars, the bullies, and worse. They are also fighting for their country.

THINKING ABOUT HOME

Everyone did it. Talked about it. *Say, these toy trains wouldn't get you anywhere back home, would they?* Or *They do have funny notions about breakfast here, don't they, nothing like back home.* After all, what was there to talk about here? The dead, the rain, the rotten food. Rumors, of course. Germans here and there, we were smashing them, no we weren't. It was a balance, thinking about home; it was necessary. To remind yourself, keep on reminding yourself who you were. That you had not always gone for three days without combing your hair. That there was another kind of life, that you had lived it.

No one talked much about going back, after. There was a superstitious reluctance to do that. But stories, memories, most of us young enough to have school pranks fresh in our minds. It too was something to hold on to.

Try to imagine this. A refugee train unloading at a station, the noise and the smell and the smoke swirling and rising, drawing your eyes to the cavernous dark roof, girders and blackness and malevolent foggy steam—don't want to look there, like looking into a nightmare under a child's bed. Now say you look down again and see a young girl, nine or ten, who looks around and around but seems to be alone in that crowd. She is wearing a dress that might once have been blue, might once have had a pattern, tiny white flowers maybe. You know that someone must have made her this dress, that it was a pretty thing; you know from the age of the girl that she probably loved it, tried it on and twirled around a warm kitchen. Probably there was a swing outside, and you can see her swinging on it, see her toes pointing in neat black shoes. What's on her feet now might be shoes, tied round and round with string to hold them. Her legs are streaked with mud and dried blood, as is every bit of her that you can see. She's clutching a baby in her arms, wrapped in bits of someone's coat; a green button winks as it catches a stray bit of light. What you can see of the baby's head is also bloody and muddy. It is very still, and you hope that it is sleeping.

The child scans the crowd, her head moves back and forth, her eyes flick here and there, but you can tell from those eyes that she doesn't expect to recognize anyone. So as you make your way to her, as you bend down so she can hear you, as you bend down to take a closer look at the bundle she is carrying, which is now making tiny mewling sounds, as you, still stooping, put an arm about her narrow shoulders and feel what you couldn't see, the way her whole body trembles as if it will never stop, as you move her with her sleepwalker's stumble toward the big red cross and whatever can be done—as you do all that, you find you are remembering a doll you had once, after Ophelia, the way you took it everywhere with you, fed it and talked to it like a real baby. That makes you remember green grass and the feeling of sunlight on your skin, someone's voice singing, a host of things. If you couldn't do that, it's hard to know what would happen. Probably you would just die for sorrow.

It's different for those who have children at home, or obligations. Mrs. Moore frets and frets about her married daughter, who is having her first baby soon. How she never liked vegetables and probably isn't watching her diet, how even a scraped knee would make her howl like the end of the world. The men show pictures and read out bits of letters they've received, all the clever and naughty things going on in a home they can walk through every time they close their eyes. Even the horrible Smythe has three little Smythes and their mother folded in his front pocket. For some there are worries about a business, is it being run all right, will the proper decisions be made while they're away. So even if they don't speak about *after*, it's always there, and home is something to go back to.

It's not the same for us. Once, on a hospital visit, there was a boy with no hands. He'd been reaching for something or someone when the shell came; he was not too badly hurt except for that. But he needed someone to write letters for him and someone to hold his cigarettes. He had beautiful hair, that boy, thick and dark and very curly. It kept tumbling over his forehead, and he kept trying to lift his arm to brush it back. "You should get someone to cut it," we said as we smoothed it back again and again. "Oh, my girl would never forgive me for that," he said. "She loves to do just what you're doing." When we held the cigarette to his lips, he seemed to kiss our fingertips.

In another bed on that ward there was a boy who was not expected to live. He was getting huge doses of morphine, but even when he was asleep his lips would twitch. When he was—not awake, he was never that—but semiconscious, he repeated a list of words over and over. Oak, beech, ash, elm, maple, oak beech ash elm maple. The boy with the beautiful hair said at first they thought he was naming trees, but then someone heard *main* and someone heard *water* and they guessed he was reciting the names of streets, the names of streets in whatever town he came from. His company had been hit hard; those who survived had been moved on, and no one in the hospital knew yet what town it was. Some of the men on the ward thought it was a small place, that he was naming every street in the town. But most of them thought it was a route he was walking. Oak-Beech-Ash-Elm-Maple-Main-Water. The way to school, maybe, or the way to his girlfriend's house. The way to his own house from the station. Over and over he walked it, Oak-Beech-Ash-Elm-Maple-Main-Water, and after a while we could see it ourselves: the tall trees leaning over the sidewalks, the shady verandas, the storefronts on Main Street, the cooler air on Water. If it was evening, we could smell the blossoms.

As the morphine wore off his voice got louder and louder, and after he'd had the next shot he'd sometimes stop suddenly, even in the middle of a word. And someone else would finish for him— -ple, Main, Water—and we realized that with everything else they were doing, or saying, or thinking, every man on that ward was walking along with him.

Our own thinking about home had that obsessive quality. Things we went over and over, trying to get the truth of. Maybe that was the difference between us and Mrs. Moore, the men with their pockets full of photographs. Home for us was not exactly something to hold on to, it was something to figure out, to understand. So many things seemed strange, there in France. It did not seem possible that our life was as we remembered it. But we both remembered it, so wasn't that some kind of proof? We were not together every minute of our childhood, of our lives, although most, perhaps. There must have been times when one of us was in a room without the other. When only one of us saw something, heard something, was spoken to. But we don't remember anything like that. This is something you have to understand, if you are to understand anything. The things we talked about in the wet tent, in the wooden room at Châlons—we shared them all. And if there was a split second, the tiniest of moments, briefer than the blink of an eye, when one of us said something—in that briefest of moments, the other had the memory, could hear, feel, taste it.

INTERVIEW

The journalist was fresh from home, and his questions made us realize how far away that was. The last thing he asked was for one thing, one experience, that would give his readers—the folks, he called them—an idea of what it was really like. So we told him about traveling on a road near Ancerville where the bombardment had been heavy a few days before. How we stopped to stretch our legs, and found a small, perfect child's hand, lying palm up in the dust.

NAN

I don't see so well now; perhaps that's why the memory pictures are so clear. Know what I mean by memory pictures? Of course you do, everybody's got them. I've been thinking about it ever since I heard. Seeing it clear as day. The path that led off the kitchen garden and down to the river. The two of them running ahead of me, trees overhanging and sunlight falling through and their feet kicking up behind them. And I thought, *Run, girls, keep running. Run right out of this.* So maybe I always knew.

I was going to leave service long ago; that was my plan. My sister had a cottage in a little place by the sea, and I was going to live there with her. Before I got too old to walk along the sand, to really live there. We grew up on an island, you see, and I always missed it. That clean wind blowing, the smell of it. So I was going to see her through the birthing, stay until they got someone else settled in. I owed them that, since they'd been so generous to me. Not *owed*, exactly, but anyway that's what I agreed to. I'd been with Miss Alice since she was a girl, and when she asked me, I couldn't say no. But one thing I've learned is that this life always has surprises in store, and most of them aren't the kind to make you jump for joy. It was the two of them who did her in. She'd never been strong, Miss Alice, but she was so lively. It was a happy house, before. Break your heart to see it happen. So I couldn't just walk away. Stayed until the girls were grown, did my best. My sister died, and I never did get to that cottage by the sea, but it's not so bad here. It took Miss Alice so long to die, poor soul, but it was written on her face from before the birth. Things changed overnight, it seemed, like the heart went out of that house, leaving nothing but a lot of echoing rooms. Even the boys changed, became sly and sad. I had to keep a sharp eye when the girls were small, even though I couldn't believe they would actually harm them. There was that business with the fountain—we never did get to the truth of that. Everyone so busy blaming that useless Susan for falling asleep.

What were they like as children? Like children, of course. They learned to walk and talk, they had tea parties for their dolls and played on the lawns. Perhaps more serious than most but that's not surprising, the house being the way it was and the mister never what you could call a warm man. I used to fancy I could tell them apart, though if you asked me I couldn't say how. Alike as two peas in a pod, they were, and if one had a stomachache the other would too, without fail. When they were small, four or five maybe, they had a special language they spoke to each other. A lot of made-up words that they seemed to understand. *Brimble* meant cake; I remember I figured that out, but as for the rest I had no idea. It used to make me a little cross, if I tell the truth, the way they would sit whispering together as if no one else mattered at all. But there, they only had each other all those years. I thought it would be good for them when they went off to Miss Reilly's school, thought they would somehow open, make lots of new friends. They did bring girls home once in a while, but not often. Still, they were good girls, never a moment's trouble. Except for the way they used to go to the river. Many a time I scolded them for that. And the day of Miss Alice's funeral, poor little mites. They adored that Miss Reilly; she has a lot to answer for, in my opinion. Always going on about the state of the world, about hunger and injustice. "Miss Reilly says women can change the world," they told me more than once. Now I don't deny this world needs some changing, but why should it be my poor girls to do it? I used to be delighted when they'd accept an invitation to a dance or a party. I'd wait up for them with a pot of cocoa, and we'd sit around the kitchen table like we used to when they were small. "Thank heaven that's over," they always said. "The silliness, Nan, you just wouldn't believe." Talking to them was like talking to one person, always was, the way they started and finished each other's sentences. I used to wonder how they would ever get married and have a normal life. It was impossible to imagine them separated like that.

They came to see me before they went away. I'd left the house, but they still came to visit me often, always brought some of that shortbread I like. They were wearing their uniforms, and very smart they looked. Sort of a greenish whipcord with blue ties and little blue hats with the brims curved down. They said there were also heavy long capes, so I didn't have to worry about them being cold. They didn't stay long; their eyes were bright as they told me about all the things they still had to gather up. I could see it was no use but I tried anyway, told them there was plenty of war work right here at home. Told them to think of their father, with James gone and only Marcus for company. They'd thought of all that, of course they had. But they were convinced that they were meant to do their bit overseas. When they left I watched them from my window, walking side by side away down the street. I felt it in my bones, and it turns out I was right. I knew I'd never see them again.

IN THE CELLAR

We met Elizabeth in the cellar of the Hotel Terminus, during an *alerte*. It was not so crowded that night. Two small children curled against their mother, so tired that only the loudest bangs made them flinch. An old woman with a maid and an ugly little dog. Several others who were huddled shapes under blankets—the staff, perhaps, who often slept in the cellar to avoid having their sleep interrupted by the journey night after night.

It was surprising that we recognized Elizabeth, for she was very changed. But we were too, which perhaps gave us eyes to recognize each other. She was fully dressed; she said that she'd been in Paris a week, waiting to be moved out again, that she'd spent so many nights shivering in her dressing gown that she'd finally decided to sleep in her clothes. We talked for a long time, speaking softly, as the children's mother had finally fallen asleep too. There was something about their pale faces, the way they breathed in unison, that broke your heart, there in the cellar.

Elizabeth was terribly thin. She said she'd had the flu, although she was much better. She said that in her last hospital there'd been a nurse who came across on a ship struck by flu. Like the worst nightmare, Elizabeth said. Like a ghost ship, people dead all over it, scores of them, barely enough left standing to sail the ship. Then we talked of our own crossing, of the time the handsome officer asked Elizabeth to dance and she vomited all down the front of his uniform, how she thought she'd die of shame. "Strange, isn't it," she said, "the things that mattered then." And we knew what she meant.

We were afraid to ask about Art, but then she told us that her mother had received word the very day we all arrived in France. Now she was trying to find the place where he was buried. "I have to do that, at least," Elizabeth said. "I can't go home and face them unless I've done that." She'd even bought a little camera to take pictures of the spot.

"I don't know how I can go home anyway," Elizabeth said. "Do you? How can we do it, how can we go back to our own table, our own beds, as if we were the same people?

"I feel broken," Elizabeth said, in the flickering candlelight in the cellar of the Hotel Terminus. "Something is broken in me. It's all just a horrible mess, and there's no meaning in any of it."

Was it right or wrong, what we did then? Holding Elizabeth's hands and telling her it was all worthwhile. That it did have meaning, that we were right to be where we were, doing what we were doing. That the world would be different, after. A better place. Was it right or wrong, at that moment, to tell Elizabeth things we no longer believed?

When the bugle sounded we made our way back up to our

rooms. There was still enough of the night left to make sleep possible, if there wasn't another *alerte*. We arranged to meet for breakfast the next day, but in the morning Elizabeth was gone and we didn't see her again.

THE SEA KING

We know, of course we know, that it's just a story Nan told. Spun out of her Irish dreams and taking hold in ours. Those long-ago nights of soft rain, in a sloping room at the top of the fragile house. But we live in a world where everything we know has been proved wrong, a world gone completely mad. If this world can exist, then anything is possible.

Nan said the Sea King lived at the deepest bottom, where only the drowned men go. He had power over the oceans and the rivers and all things that moved upon them. And the schools of swimming fish were his spies and messengers, bringing back news from the farthest reaches of his kingdom. He was fierce and angry, and the gates of his palace were built from dead men's bones. A mound of skulls guarded his treasure room, chests filled with gold and jewels from ships he had caused to sink. Sometimes a chest broke open as it spiraled slowly down to the depths, and the sea floor for miles around the palace was littered with precious stones that glowed in the greenish light. The Sea King's children played games with those gems, arranging them in intricate patterns that could be glimpsed if you looked down through clear water on a still, sunny day. There were also beautiful necklaces that had hung around the necks of drowned women, and they floated gently down to that quiet place.

In Nan's stories the Sea King brought nothing but storms and death, his rage against the world. But in a world gone mad, a world where everything had been proved wrong, we wondered if that was too. Perhaps his kingdom was a beautiful, gentle place, his wrath really sorrow, pining for lost children who had disappeared into the world of men. Perhaps that's who we are, perhaps we are really the Sea King's beautiful daughters. Lost, long lost, wandering ill at ease through the world of foggy air.

CLASSMATES

We ran into them in Paris, the way you ran into people you knew in the war. Sitting at a table outside the Café de la Paix, across from the Opéra. Weren't we surprised to see them there, with their hair cut short, just like ours. Though when I think of it, back home they used to help out in soup kitchens and raise money for things, so perhaps it was not so strange that they came to the war. They had only three nights in Paris, and they'd already spent two down in the Gare du Nord, helping with refugee trains and feeding soldiers. We went on to Rumpelmayer's for tea and ice cream—very watery, as usual—and then they came back to the Hive for the evening. Marjorie played her funny little piano a bit, and Jess and Molly from across the hall popped in, and we had a grand time, talking about old friends. It was quite astonishing how many had turned up in Paris.

They were the same as always, maybe a little more so. Quiet, I mean. How I envied them, being up close to the front. Marjorie and I worked at the refugee center, and it's not that our work wasn't important. Finding clothes for the poor things and a place to stay, whatever bits of furniture we could lay our hands on. Scrambling always to find *essence* for the old car we drove around in. But somehow it didn't feel like really being in the war, I don't know why. It certainly looked like it—soldiers everywhere and all the statues sandbagged, shopwindows taped. The dark streets at night, only an occasional dim blue light. No hot water except on Saturday, no coffee, no meat most days. But all the restaurants and cafés were open, shows at night, people filling the streets—it was all such *fun*. Even when the big gun boomed, you would see people flinch, then shrug and carry on, maybe checking their watch to see how long before the next shell. We were all mad to go to the front, to see it, and we hoped to arrange an excursion. I remember how they looked when we said that. It reminded me of our school days, how they always seemed a little too good for the world. Not snobbish, I don't mean that at all. But you know how when you get a couple hundred girls together, there are always rivalries and tiffs and dramas. Well, they were never drawn into any of that; I don't remember a single time. They always kept themselves apart, always seemed to have a certain standard of behavior. I've often thought that this world must have been a constant disappointment to them.

YELLOW LEAVES

We weren't expecting the noise. Could have had no idea how it would be. Not the guns and explosions when near the front, that's a particular agony, and an undertone even when far away. But more the constant ruckus, living in a large group of people. The shouting in the camp, the singing and sounds of hammering. Horses and motors and airplanes if they're near. The racket in the canteen or mess hall, always something. There's no place for contemplation, no space for it, every waking moment and many sleeping ones filled up with sound.

On our last morning at home we woke early and went to sit in the silence on the kitchen porch. A cold morning, the grass rimed with frost that was beginning to glisten as the sun touched it. The distant line of silent, colored hills. We didn't speak, just tried to take it in, our stomachs in nagging, queasy knots that eased a little as the sun reached the spot where we sat. It was completely still, no sound from the sleeping house behind us, no bird or animal.

But then there *was* a sound, we gradually became aware of it, a wrenching, tearing, rattling sound, becoming louder and more constant as we listened. It sounded like—something, yet like nothing we'd ever heard before. Then we saw a flicker of movement and understood what was happening. As the sun warmed the frosted yellow maples that ringed the back garden, the leaves began to detach with a snap, fall with an icy clatter. First one, then another, then more and more, a shower. On our last morning we realized that we had been living in a silence so absolute that we could hear the sound each leaf made as it fell.

It can never be like that again. This is the sound of the modern world, the world we are fighting for. The *tramp-tramp-tramp* of a thousand feet marching, the jingle of harnesses and medals. The shriek of train whistles, the rattle of a clean gun being assembled, the howls of men in pain.

LETTER

Dear Anne,

Thank you for your last letter, and all the news of home. It's good to be reminded. We feel so far away in this new life we are living. As you see, the black pen is working beautifully. It's a pity the paper doesn't do it justice.

We were glad to hear that Father was well when last you saw

him. He writes that the business is booming, and to tell you the truth, we are dismayed that someone so close to us is growing rich out of all this suffering. Father would say that's the way of the world, but surely that's what we are fighting to change.

We are just back from a few days' leave in Paris. You wouldn't recognize the place. Soldiers and sandbags everywhere, shopwindows taped up. Taxis charge exorbitant rates after dark, and it's difficult to find your way at night with only the blue lights marking the shelters. But the cafés and restaurants are full, and life goes on, even though every second person you see is dressed in mourning. We met up with Jane and Marjorie and spent a pleasant evening in their apartment, which they call the Hive because they've painted everything yellow and black. They are working hard at one of the refugee centers but still having a grand time—you remember they were such jolly girls. It must be gratifying to know that so many of your old girls are here, doing their bit with the same spirit that carried us through all those marches and rallies. Let anyone who still doubts women's capabilities just see what we are doing, over here and at home, in this time of crisis.

We sometimes wonder if we could better serve by helping with the refugees, who number in the thousands, pitiful souls, often with nothing more than the clothes on their backs. Or in a hospital, where the work the nurses and doctors are doing is nothing short of heroic. We constantly feel that there should be more we can do. But we know our work is important too. It was explained to us on our first day that we are here to provide a civilizing influence in the camp, an alternative to the filthy estaminets and the women who appear wherever soldiers are gathered. And the men appreciate what we do for them. We get to know some; they tell us about their lives back home, and we wonder what happens to them when they leave. It is horrible to think that many will have been wounded or killed. The front is moving closer, and we often hear the guns and think of the men out there fighting. The camp is on standby, ready to move at a moment's notice, which is very hard on the nerves.

We have just received word that there is to be a dance tonight. Of all our duties this is the most onerous. The dances are held every few weeks in a nearby camp, and though canteen workers and sometimes nurses are brought in from miles around, there are never nearly enough women for the hundreds of men. The room is bright and rather hot and smelly from all the people packed in. Usually there's a Victrola, sometimes a real band. A whistle blows every two minutes to change partners, and occasionally there are terrible fights. All for two minutes' shuffle around the floor with a woman in your arms. For that's what we are at these times, Women, not ourselves at all. It is a most disheartening experience, and no matter how many times we are assured that it is important for morale we can't help thinking, as we pull our aching heads and feet into the truck for the ride home, that it's not at all what we came to France for.

Two weeks ago we saw our first Germans, wounded prisoners in the hospital where we help out on our free day. The strange thing was they were just like our boys, frightened and in pain. So young. They were excited that we spoke some German, for they speak no English, and only one knows a little French. We helped one write a letter to his mother—heaven knows if she'll ever receive it—and you know, it was so much like the letters we write for our boys, full of the same concerns and reassurances. Many of the men say they hate the generals who run the war far more than the "enemy." Oh, sometimes this war seems like a terrible machine, carried along by its own momentum. Chewing up lives and spitting them out. We do our work day by day and try not to think about the enormity of it. The destruction, the horror, the waste. It seems like it will go on and on, until there are no young men left in the world. We wonder then if we did the right thing by coming here, by being part of it.

SAINTE GERMAINE

In Bar sur Aube we asked Hugh what it was like.

"Boring," he said. "If it wasn't for the terror, we'd all be bored to death.

"It's hard to explain," he said. "Like a dream, it's something like a dream. I don't mean like a nightmare, not just that. But things have their own logic, things operate by their own rules, and it makes some kind of sense at the front, although it would make none at all in the real world."

We were sitting at a little table on a narrow white-walled street. Hugh had persuaded us that we needed an outing on our free day, that we needed to get right away from the war. He said he would organize everything. We had stopped asking or even wondering how Hugh was always able to lay his hands on things. Old cars or bicycles or new bars of soap. Something close to real coffee, day passes. He just seemed to manage, that's how it was with him.

The street was off the shady town square, where three or four women chatted by the ancient well. Now and then they would shake their heads, hand on cheek.

"This should be what's real," Hugh said. "What's been forever, what will go on long after we're gone."

Another woman had come to the well, was drawing up water,

and we knew he was thinking of the deep grooves we'd noticed in the gray stone, how many hundreds of years it had taken bucket ropes to make them. But we also noticed that the chatting women seemed to register the other's presence without pausing in their conversation or turning their heads. To our eyes, she looked like one of them. About the same age, dressed in much the same way. Nothing, to our eyes, explained why the little group turned away from her without actually moving. She seemed oblivious, yet the set of her back as she walked away showed she was not. And we thought how Hugh's words meant this as well.

We went a few miles out of the town to swim, to a place where the river eddied in a deep green pool. We changed in the trees, thankful for the frivolous impulse, long ago and far away, that made us squeeze our swimming costumes into our bulging trunks. When we emerged from the trees, Hugh said, "Good God, even the scars match," and we looked down at our pale legs, the paler web of lines. We might have shown him then how the scars didn't quite match, but he turned away quickly, embarrassed, we supposed, to be looking.

It was one of the things we liked about Hugh, the way he didn't ever play that tedious game of trying to tell us apart. Most people did, and had done all our lives. As if together we were too much for them, as if the only way they could deal with us was to divide, diminish us. But Hugh had always accepted us just as we were, just as we were with each other.

Soldiers loved to play the guessing game. Our first day at the canteen, Mrs. Moore gave us a talk. "Girls," she said, "you must always remember that these boys don't expect to see their old age, and many of them won't. So we have to make some . . . allowances. Of course I don't mean anyone has to put up with any real unpleasantness. But we must try not to be shocked if their behavior, their conversation, is not always what we would demand in our own parlors."

Dear Mrs. Moore, with her friend Dr. Thomas who came discreetly calling, and Colonel McAndrew not so long after the doctor was sent home. We remembered her words, we consciously made allowances those first weeks, before we grew our skin. But one night there was a mood in the canteen. An edge to the laughter, to the tone of the voices. Most of the men were going up to the line the next day and drifted away early, but twenty or thirty lingered, playing our two records over and over. A few of them were standing about near our counter, and one of them came over and said, "My friends don't believe I can tell you apart, will you help me out?"

We said all right, and smiled when we said it, remembering Mrs. Moore and thinking that though we were heartily sick of this game, it was little enough to do for this poor boy, on what might well be his last evening on earth. He had a mess of short red hair, that boy, and very pale eyelashes. One eye seemed noticeably smaller than the other, and on his cheek beneath it was a dark brown mole. He didn't look old enough to shave, but there was a reddish stubble on his chin.

His friends drew closer as he gave us directions. "Turn away from me, right around. Now turn back, look at me. Smile. Frown. Reach up, pretend you're taking pins from your hair. Touch your cheeks together, yes, that's good. Stay like that. Now touch each other's cheeks, but slowly, very slowly."

His tongue came out to lick his bottom lip. The record needle had come to the end of the long, long trail and hissed and scratched, and that seemed to be the only sound. "Now," he said, and we wondered why we had thought him a boy when the look in his mismatched eyes was ancient, "Now—" We said, "Time's up," and turned away, busying ourselves with things behind the counter, laughing as if it had all been harmless.

Willows grew on the far bank and dappled the light on the surface of the river. It was marvelous to be swimming, and we laughed and splashed and ducked each other, and Hugh swam beneath us and tickled the soles of our feet. We stayed in the water after he climbed out, and he watched us, lying on the grassy bank, smoking a cigarette and looking completely contented. We floated on our backs, on our stomachs, arms and legs splayed, and dived down to see if we could reach the bottom. And there was something magical in that green underwater light, in the fronded weeds that waved and beckoned us down. It was deeper than we thought; our hair floated free behind us, and we reached out a hand to each other; fingertips skimmed, and missed.

And then there was a moment of panic. Cold, as if the water itself had chilled and darkened, inexplicable. We kicked to the surface, flailed our way to the bank where Hugh lounged, felt the sun begin to warm us again, our racing hearts slow down. We didn't speak of it.

"So, kids," Hugh said, squinting against the smoke rising from his cigarette, "how did you get those scars?" We surprised ourselves by telling him. It was one of those things we didn't talk about except to each other. From a time we didn't talk about either, except to each other. The summer our mother died, the day our brothers were allowed to go to the party and we were not. We prowled the garden in a rage, hitting at things with sticks and stones, and shattered a pane of glass that guarded the tomatoes, and then shattered more; the sound become intoxicating. Sometime later we sat on the grass facing each other, toe to toe, and drew on our skin with a shard of that glass, copying the moves exactly. Blood rolled down to pool in our folded stockings. Oh what a fuss when Nan found us. It hurt then, and later, but the wounds healed quickly, leaving identical scars. Identical but reversed, of course, from sitting toe to toe.

"What's it like?" Hugh asked later. It was so peaceful there in the sunlight. The only sound the wind through the trees, a bell far away.

"It's safe," we said.

"No matter what happens, you're not alone," we said.

"Isn't that supposed to be God?" he said.

Then Hugh said that of everyone over here he probably felt sorriest for the chaplains, and then he told us about the old aunt who'd raised him, the widow of his father's brother, and how he had scars himself, from the whippings. She used a switch, willow maybe, and they had to pray on their knees before and after. But he said he never could hold it against her. Because after a whipping she'd go to her room and he'd hear her. Muffled, like her face was in a pillow, which it likely was. Sobbing as if her heart would break.

"She wasn't a cruel woman," Hugh said. "She was doing what she truly believed had to be done. And it tormented her."

We asked about his parents, but he said he didn't know much

about them, had never even seen a picture. His aunt told him they had just died, but he never quite believed her. He threw himself back, hands beneath his head, and spoke to the sky, to the over-hanging trees.

"I was five or six when I came to her, and I don't remember any-thing at all before that. Strange, isn't it? Five or six years is a long time, you'd think there'd be something. Their faces looking at me, the sound of their voices."

Once he heard his aunt telling a woman from the church that he'd lived just like a Gypsy, and he got the idea that his parents really were Gypsies, that they'd somehow misplaced him and one day would look around and realize he was missing, come back for him. And they'd all drive away together in a brightly painted cara-van, pulled by a horse named Old Joe.

"And every morning, early, I'd hear the milkman's horse and think—well, you know," Hugh said. "Her husband was a parson, and after he died she must have thought her life would go a certain way. But she took me in, so it went another way. What was that like for her? She knew nothing about children, she had no . . . imagina-tion. And I was a handful, no question. I fought her all the way. It wasn't easy.

"Time we were going," Hugh said in his poshest voice. "We have reservations at a charming little inn nearby."

When he sat up we saw the marks on his back, and without thinking we reached out to touch them. His skin shuddered be-neath our fingers, and we snatched them back. And asked how he could be so understanding.

"Oh, there was my friend Tom," he said. "I met him very soon after I came there, in this dusty little lane behind our houses. He laughed at the clothes she'd put me in, but then he said I could share his parents, as I didn't have my own. That's the kind of fellow Tom was, even then. And I suppose I did share his family, in a way. Certainly his house always felt more like home to me. They were a grand bunch—well, they still are, of course. So much laughter. So I was lucky, you see. I always had that to balance things, to show me there was another way. Otherwise—well, who knows."

Hugh really did know of an inn nearby; we sat outside on the edge of a great cliff with the fan-shaped Aube valley spread out below us. The small square fields in shades of green and yellow and the white road snaking north. There were omelettes and sausages, salad, and it all tasted wonderful, in a way you could understand only if you'd spent time picking lumps of gristle from a mess tin. We all grew giddy on the local wine and looked down the valley as the light began to fade.

Hugh said the place was the cliff of Sainte Germaine, and he told us the story, though not how he'd learned it. How long ago the conqueror Attila was camped on top of the cliff, right where we were now giggling and eating. He sent word down to the town of Bar to bring their prettiest girl up to him or he would destroy them all. So a beautiful girl named Germaine came up the steep path, slowly and steadily, but when she reached the top, before anyone could stop her or even guess what was in her mind, she broke and ran, throwing herself over the cliff to the valley far below.

It was easy to imagine it in that place, as the light began to fade and ancient shadows appeared. The girl climbing through them, her breath coming harder as she went. Hearing the sounds of the camp as she came nearer, probably not so different from those of a modern army camp at rest. Knowing that this was happening to her simply because she was a girl, because she was pleasing to look at, which should not have been a bad thing. The flames of the torches, as she drew nearer, the bellowing of animals. The escape.

We talked then about whether it took more courage to live or to die in such a situation. And argued a little; Hugh said one should always choose life, that was the only way for the human spirit to triumph.

"Otherwise," he said, "the bravest and the best are dying every day. Otherwise there'll only be scoundrels like me left to run the world."

As we stood to go, we asked Hugh if there was some kind of stone or marker at the place where Sainte Germaine leaped.

"No idea," he said. "Maybe I made it all up."

And we chased him all the way back to the motor car.

On the drive we slept; it was completely dark. I woke once, and the two of them were laughing at something I hadn't heard.

HUGH

And what did Hugh want? It should have been a simple thing. He wanted a quiet place, that was all. A place where he didn't have to do anything, be anything, a place where he could just lay his head down. He wanted to be close to something soft and human.

He thought of Tom's older sisters sometimes, the way he ran in and out of their lives all his childhood, the way they always made a space for him. Stopped whatever they were doing to smile, to say "Hello, Hugh," sometimes offer a big hug when he was smaller. The wonder of what they had to give him.

There was a girl back home who tried. Wrote letters about missing him, asked questions he couldn't possibly answer. She wanted to know what it was like, she wanted to be able to picture him day by day. How could he tell her anything at all? It wasn't the thought of the censors that stopped him, it was that she would have to be there to even begin to imagine it, and even then she wouldn't have believed it. He couldn't believe it himself. He knew there must have been stages; it didn't all happen at once. He and Tom sitting in their secret place on the riverbank, the cave they'd made when they were boys, from shrubs and low-hanging branches. There was still a rotting bit of mat on the ground, and he remembered how at one time they'd rolled it up and hidden it in a hole they'd dug beneath an old log, how they carefully wiped out their footprints with a fanned branch kept for that purpose. They went there, alone or together, through their childhood, eating sweet things filched from Tom's house, making fishing poles and lures, carving bits of wood with the knives they were not allowed to have. It filled him with wonder, always, that people could pass by and not notice the notch in the tree trunk; that they would assume, if they thought about it at all, that the log had fallen just so, that the fanned branch was like any other. That, if you didn't know what to expect, you would never think to look for it.

The afternoon he and Tom decided to join up, they sat outside the cave drinking bottles of beer, too big now to be comfortable hunched inside. They accused each other of leaving the mat out, the mat he had taken from his aunt's spare room and never been questioned about, for she wouldn't imagine he would want such a thing. It had been years since either had been there; neither would admit to being the last. Hugh wondered sometimes if other boys had found the place, would wonder themselves about that bit of cloth and who had brought it there. But he knew it was already earth-colored, already rotted to nothing.

And he knew there must have been stages, between that afternoon and this. The crisp autumn sky above them, the sound of the river, so close yet only glimpsed from where they sat. He couldn't have gone straight from that to this creature in the line, who was so incredibly weary. The rank smell of himself that he no longer noticed but assumed. The foul taste in his mouth, the itching and grime all over his body, his hands thickened and scarred, fingernails blackened from bangs and injuries he hadn't even noticed. The girl at home knit him warm stockings and thick pullovers the color of smoke. He wiggled and yanked the boots from his foul, soupy feet, peeled or sometimes cut off the old socks and pulled on the new. He thought of her fleetingly then, thought that whatever she imagined, stitch by stitch in the lamp glow, it could never be this, could never come close to this.

All he wanted was something simple, and he thought for a while he'd found it. The first night in camp he went to the canteen, not wanting to spend another evening in an estaminet, with rough wine and bragging soldiers' talk. The canteen was crowded, thick with smoke and mugs of cocoa, a record playing, gingham curtains at the windows. He found himself a corner with a pile of old magazines and tried to settle himself to read, but there was a restlessness in him, a twitching, and he thought maybe a glass of wine after all. Then he saw them behind the counter, standing side by side, and in the same instant they each raised an arm, brushed the hair from their foreheads with the back of a hand, and something in that paired gesture brought a great peace to settle on him, as if it was something he'd been waiting to see all his life.

When the canteen closed a couple of men stayed behind to help tidy up and he stayed too, and when all the chairs were straightened, the dirty mugs collected, they all sat around in the little kitchen area, perched on chairs and crates, talking about nothing in particular. He lay down to sleep that night feeling cleaner than he had in years. And that became the pattern of his evenings. The camp was in a dip, surrounded by low hills, and after supper he would walk a particular path, sit down on a particular rock, smoke a cigarette and watch the light fade from the untouched hills. Sometimes he could hear the guns faintly, but that only made it more peaceful. Then back down to the canteen and always, after the men drifted away, the three of them left talking.

When he went back up to the line they were in a quiet sector, firing over the top once in a while to remind themselves there was a war on, and he thought—for his aunt must have had some influence—that it was because he'd been living so purely. He thought if he'd seen one woman raise a hand to her forehead it would have been the same old story, but it was all different because they were two. He found he even looked around in a different way, storing up things to tell them the next time he went back. He loved to make them laugh, but he also loved the melancholy that was part of their containment, part of the seriousness that made him feel that when they spoke together they were really talking, not just exchanging words. He told them things about himself that he might have told other people, but in a different way entirely, and he thought it was the same for them. When the Armistice came he was far away, and then he was sent to Germany, and that was where he saw the old newspaper. And he wasn't exactly surprised, but it still broke his heart.

ABOUT THE SENTRY

He was never quite the same. Not that it changed his life, not that it made him crazy or restless or morose. Or not any more than he already was. But of all the things he'd seen—and he'd seen enough to give the whole world nightmares—it was the thing that stayed with him. Not the thing that he talked about over a jug or, more rarely, lying in the dark with his wife, but the thing that stayed with him. The thing he couldn't shake, the thing on his mind when his eyes snapped open, heart pounding. One minute he was hiding a smoke in his cupped hand, stamping his feet as he walked and thinking only that he was cold, that he'd be glad to get down below to the steamy light. Then nothing was ever the same.

He blamed himself. He'd seen it time and again, some fellow with days or hours to go who let his breath out a bit, started to think he'd made it. Let himself think about a chair by the fire, soft hands, loved faces. And then *wham* and home all right, but in a shape no one would recognize. So he blamed himself, but who could have known that it would come like that, the thing that would do it for him? Not that it changed his life. But how could he know? When he first saw the woman who would be his wife, she was wearing a long dark dress that billowed in a cold wind.

He never talked about it, though there were times when he was close. And he thought the worst part was the way they looked right past him. Changed his life and never even noticed he was there.

NEAR THE FIELD OF CROSSES

We all have those pictures in our heads. Those moments of memory caught and held, for some reason, and perhaps if we could string them all together they would make some sense of our lives. Not for anyone else but for ourselves, since the moments we hold would have been passed by anyone else, on their way to their own collection. Little things. The way the light fell on a certain wall, the dappled shadow dancing there. Drops of dew glistening on a blowsy orange flower. The way the wind shifts before a storm, exposing the undersides of leaves, the way the lamplight strikes a particular face, or the intense, wonderful melancholy of certain notes on a piano. Each cross in this field marks a nest of those kind of memories, along with whatever is left of the person who enclosed it. And no one could ever guess, not even the closest person, just what those moments would be. Should that be chilling, or liberating?

Once, you see, I would have known that ours were shared. How can you imagine what this sudden uncertainty is like? There is a memory that I know is mine alone. Waking suddenly in a dark car, and she and Hugh were laughing, together.

IN THE EVENING

I went to meet Hugh. Such a simple thing to say, five little words. But oh, the chasm that opened up. I went to meet Hugh and it changed everything. I can't even say why I went, what I expected. Only that it seemed a way to end the turmoil. When we drove back from the place of Sainte Germaine it was very dark, and Hugh had to drive slowly and carefully. Ruth fell asleep in the back, and maybe it was the wine, I don't know, I don't have much experience of wine. We were talking, Hugh and I, in a dark bubble moving through a dark sea of night, and suddenly I felt such a great opening up. And I realized, I think right then I realized, that it was because Hugh was talking to *me*. I don't think I can explain what that was like.

I knew the way he walked, each evening after supper; I had watched him. I waited until Ruth uncapped her pen, straightened the notepaper on the writing board, and then I said, "I think I'll go for a bit of a stroll." She raised her eyes, faintly puzzled; perhaps my voice sounded as strange as it did to my own ears. And then I was outside and then I was walking the path that led up, out of the camp, and my thoughts wheeled like a flock of startled birds. I settled myself to wait by the big rock that split the path in two, and I waited and waited, but he didn't come.

It was nearly dark when I came down, the canteen already bustling. "Sorry, I lost track of time," I said, and the lie lay, an ugly thing between us. Hugh didn't appear that night, but we saw him with his kit the next morning. His eyes were red and there was a big discolored swelling high on one cheek. "Knew I shouldn't have gone to Papa George's bar," he said. And with a wave of his hand he was gone, falling in with a line of marching men, marching down the rutted road and out of our lives. Leaving me with a broken thing to try to put together.

ARMISTICE

Suddenly it was all over. A cold, misty day like so many others, breaking up packing cases to feed the fire. All morning the guns roared without pause; eleven o'clock came and went and we thought it had just been another rumor. But then gradually, so gradually, they stopped, and then there was silence. Berthe paused in her stirring and said, *"C'est fini?"* Then she sank to the ground with her apron covering her eyes and huge sobs shaking her shoulders.

Later we bounced to town in a truck filled with laughing soldiers, riding up front with Corporal Easton. Every so often he would bang the steering wheel with the heel of his hand, give his shoulders a twitch, and say, "It's over, it's really over."

The main square was still thronged with people, some crying, some dancing. There were uniforms everywhere, and women in black, and children darting through the crowd playing tag. All the windows around the square were open, and in each was a row of lighted candles. We had thought to treat ourselves to a meal, but every café was filled with drunken soldiers, singing and crashing glasses and bottles. A group had commandeered the town's only taxi and was screeching through the narrow streets, whooping and firing revolvers in the air. Others staggered by with their arms around local girls or each other. It was not a place for us, and we finally managed to find a ride back to camp. We thought at least we would sleep, really sleep, but our dreams were filled with dead men.

TEACUP

When our papers came we didn't know what to think. Now it was over, it was all over. We were no longer necessary, were about to be spun loose. Into what, we wondered, and couldn't imagine. Since the Armistice we had been moved from camp to camp as they closed down, and that was part of the strangeness. We missed Berthe's humming, little Albert's grin as he dumped a stack of kindling on the kitchen floor. The faces of men we'd come to know. The work was the same, the big kettles of cocoa, of coffee, the piles of cigarettes and chocolate bars. But the mood was different, the men restless and eager to be gone. They chafed at the regulations they were still forced to live by, cursed the drilling that filled up their days. There were always fights. Men who had fought side by side now plowed their fists into each other at the slightest excuse. Was this the new world?

And between ourselves there was a strangeness, and that was the worst part. Since I went to meet Hugh, since I lied. Once Mrs. Moore got a letter saying that her father had suffered a stroke, and Dr. Thomas explained it over lunch. He said it was a severing in the brain, and that was what this felt like. An emptiness and a terrible thrumming panic. We were no longer whole; we couldn't imagine how we would ever be whole again. We thought of Nan's favorite teacup, the one with the little blue flowers around the rim. She dropped it once and it split in two, and she spent an evening with a pot of glue and a matchstick, putting it back together. She still used it after—it still held tea—but you could always see the join.

JOURNEY

The little train stood in the station, the few freight cars still bearing the legend *40 hommes 8 chevaux.* The platform was crowded: soldiers with their heavy packs, people with bags and bundles. Perhaps we felt it as we put our feet on the step, pulled with tired arms, but everyone was laughing and waving and pushing and there was no time to say *Stop. Wait.* No way to turn back against the bodies behind to say *No, we won't go.* Pushed into our seat. The final click of the doors, our shoulders bumping hard, and the knowledge dawning with our exhaled breath that we were caught up in another thing, by another thing. The signs were still posted in the carriage: *Taisez-vous, méfiez-vous, les oreilles ennemies vous écoutent.* We spoke in whispers, if we spoke at all.

So hot on the train, no air. Crammed together, the smells rising from all those bodies, wet wool and worse, much worse. Impossible to open a window, to even see through a window while the rain slashed down. Cold, hard rain. There was a time in our life when it was wonderful to sit in a window seat and watch the rain. Books in our laps, the feel of paper at our fingertips, and raising our eyes again and again to look through to the dripping trees, the garden. It was possible then to imagine any hero appearing, water dripping from his cape, from his hat, as he looked up at our white shapes in the window. It was possible then to spend an entire day with the fire hissing, the gentle rain falling, the gray light slowly deepening. Dreaming. On the train we understood that there were no heroes, that such a life could not possibly be ours.

The journey took two days. The train crawled slowly, sometimes reversing for miles, sometimes sitting motionless for an hour or more. We passed through villages blasted to piles of rubble, the burned-out shells of trucks, the splintered remains of horse-drawn carts. The roads we could see were filled with lines of people walking with heads down, shoulders hunched against the rain. They had the look of people who had been walking forever, who would never reach their destination.

There was a soldier sitting beside us; he named the battlefields we passed near. His foot was bandaged, crutches leaning against the seat. "I hurt it playing football yesterday," he said. "My only war wound, can you believe it?"

He showed us photographs of his girlfriend, of his parents and younger brother. We saw our own hands reaching out to take them, heard our own voices, but all the time there was a terrible pounding in our heads.

Toward evening of the first day the rain stopped, and the train moved into the night. And it was like that, moving *into* night, as if it were a strange new country. We had dinner tickets but we let them fall to the muddy floor, the bright green paper soon an unrecognizable mass. When the soldier returned from the dining car he fell asleep, his head lolling back, his mouth open. Dreaming, no doubt, of his girlfriend's soft arms, his mother's apple pie. Soon everyone was asleep, the carriage filled with exhaled breath while we watched through the window.

"What can we do?" I whispered to our reflections. "What can we ever do?"

Ruth reached for my hand and we held on to each other as we moved through the country called night.

The next day the countryside was untouched by war but still dead and colorless beneath a lowering sky. When we finally reached Bordeaux everything sped up around us, the crowds at the station, the docks. Faces looming and receding—a woman's fat cheeks, her mouth opening and closing soundlessly; a man's bushy eyebrows; the red lines on the back of the taxi driver's neck. We were swept along, our feet so heavy we could barely put one in front of the other. The ship rearing up, impossibly huge, our hands on the grimy rope of the gangway.

DR. MAITLAND

Someone told me they needed my attention, and when they didn't appear at dinner I went looking, knocked at their cabin door. They were agitated when I entered. One—I don't know which—was pacing back and forth, her hands in her hair. One was sitting at the tiny writing desk, scribbling on pieces of paper that fell to the floor as I closed the door behind me. I introduced myself, and the pacing one sat down on the edge of the bunk, folding her hands in her lap. I asked how they were and they said they were very tired, that they hadn't slept for the two days it took the train to reach Bordeaux. They said there was a terrible racket in their heads, that if they could just sleep, maybe it would stop. They asked if I knew when the ship would sail, and I said that I understood it would be within the hour. I gave them a mild sedative and said I would come back in the morning. I've thought about it since, and I don't think there's any way I could have known. You can't imagine what it was like, the stress we'd all been living under. To be suddenly on the verge of a normal life. The cruel limbo of the sea voyage. Everyone on that ship was in distress, and I couldn't have known what they would do.

THE DEEP

Without each other we are in pieces, we are scattered to the wide winds. These past weeks we are put together like the broken teacup. In the train our shoulders bumped and we felt those rough edges grating. Nothing feels as it did; we have to find a way back.

There is a terrible racket in our heads. In the cabin we pace and pace, and our hearts beat loudly, thrumming to our fingertips. We are the same age our mother was when we were born.

The doctor comes with soothing powders, but we are beyond that. She says with a smile that in a few days we'll be home again, as if that should mean something. We pace and pace, holding ourselves together. Bits of us straining to break loose; we will be scattered.

The ship moves off with a lurch, and we pace and pace. We are trapped now, there's a terrible pounding in our heads. The light-house sends its beam through the cabin, a darting streak of light, and we know at once what we have to do.

TESTIMONY OF THE SENTRY

Walter Allingham, 339th Field Artillery, was stationed in the bow on Sunday night. He saw two young women walking along the deck toward him at about seven o'clock. It was so dark he could not see what they wore, except what appeared to be big cloaks that blew out in the wind. They were talking to each other and stopped when they reached the bow on the port side. Suddenly one of them placed her foot on the rail and scrambled over it, jumped into the water. The other followed almost immediately. Neither screamed nor made any noise, and the splash when they struck the water was drowned by the noise of the tide rushing along the ship's sides.

AFTER

Here there are two tall windows, and the gauzy white curtains lift and fall like a breath, like a sigh. The sounds that reach us are muffled, and we wonder if someone has died.

HOUR OF LEAD

This is what Amelia thought in the space of the spoon, in the space between the *tap-tap* on the edge of the bowl and the light touch on her lower lip. She thought, *I must get out of here;* she thought, *I will never get out of here.*

The spoon reminded her of things, and it reminded her of being reminded. How one time, washing the curved handle of an old baby spoon, she had suddenly smelled wood smoke, had seen her mother's hand and the shadowed place where her face was, light bursting all around. This, she believed, was her earliest memory. And that reminded her of another time, feeding Raymond in his chair. How he kept grabbing at the spoon, laughing and splattering food about, and how she had finally shouted and banged it down with great force. His sudden round eyes and the crackle of the letter in her apron pocket as she scooped him up and held him close, both of them howling then. It was the letter, of course, it was Hugh, of course; it always was in those days.

She told Raymond everything in his first long months, while he kicked his fat legs in the crib or banged pots together, sitting on the kitchen floor. Crooned Hugh's name through the darkest part of the night, rocking him back to sleep. Until, having told it all, she found that she could fold it up and put it away, like the letters, stumble across it only now and then, as she did with them, in the time that was the rest of her life.

She wondered who would find the letters now, and what they would make of them. Perhaps nothing; you had to read between the lines, after all. You had to know the look of the hand that held the pen, the exact way the lips would move with the words; you had to know what came before and after. Still, there were times when it had mattered a great deal that someone would know about them. The envelopes with the Bolivian stamps cut off—what had she done with those? The letters themselves in another long envelope marked *Bills*. The disintegrating rubber bands that she replaced each time she came across them.

Once she bought a new coat, fine dark green wool, and when one of her granddaughters came to visit, she said, "Try it on, see how it looks." The girl slipped her arms into the sleeves, shook her long hair free of the collar, and Amelia stood behind her, lifting the last strands of hair and looking at their reflections in the mirror on the opened door. "It suits you, that coat," she said. "You should have it, after."

All the time thinking that she would slip the letters into the pockets, that the girl would find them, think about them, puzzle it out. She meant to do it the next day, but that was years ago and she had no idea if she really had. Now the girl lived in another country, didn't she? With a husband and dark-eyed children. And who knew what had happened to that fine green coat, what had happened to her shoes, to all those other things she no longer had a use for. The letters could be anywhere or nowhere, but it didn't matter in the same way; she realized she had let them go sometime, without even noticing. And she thought how it seemed to get easier and easier as you got older, this unburdening. When she had moved to an apartment from the old house, her sons had minded, her grandchildren more, but she herself had not felt a thing as she closed the heavy front door.

Her husband had a kind face, a small mustache. When he asked if he might see her again there was something in his voice, his eyes, that said it would be a serious business. The girl she had been would have run from that, to a dance or a stroll by the lake. A few years before, she would have told him no and moved on without pause, as if the question had nothing at all to do with her. But a few years before, the people she loved were all still alive. Her mother and father, Beattie and Archie and Tom.

She had always thought Archie a bit of a fool, just one of the boys singing silly songs on someone's veranda. But then he died in the mud with her picture in his pocket, and she thought that she might have loved him. And then Beattie with the baby in her arms, and Tom so soon after. Her mother dropped a cup in the kitchen; it fell so slowly that Amelia could see every shift, every half-turn in the air, a few drops of tea spinning out like something much thicker. Her mother knew from that moment, and when they finally came to tell her she only nodded, caught her breath with one jagged, tearing sound.

Tom's last letter came the next day, like something out of a dream. *My dearest little sister,* he wrote, *for you will always be that to me. . . .* Going on to tell her the usual things about his strange routine, the noise of the big guns. At the end of the letter he told her not to worry so much, that he had this feeling he would be all right. She was astonished that he could be so wrong.

Hugh went to war too; he lived, but did not come back. It seemed that she had known him forever, known him since he and Tom were inseparable, going off on mysterious journeys with willow whips in their hands and their caps askew. Chasing her away when she tried to follow. She was wild in those days, climbing to the tops of trees. Her hair a tangle and her stockings always torn, her mother's despair. The boys teased her terribly and once, in a rage, she threw a tin shovel that caught Hugh near the eye, making him bleed. His face went pale but he didn't make a sound, only turned and walked carefully back to the house where her mother and Ada clucked and patched him. Amelia was sent to her room for the rest of the day, watching the changing light in a stupor of fear and shame.

Hugh lived with an old aunt, a parson's widow who was always trying to beat the Lord into him. Or so Tom said, and it may have been true; he was always at their house, and their father didn't seem to mind. Teased him and gave him chores to do, just like Tom, and lectured him too when they'd been caught at something. Like the time they rigged a bucket of kitchen slops in the pear tree over the swing, soaking Beattie and her new beau. Poor Beattie had been so furious, the three of them listening outside the door to her loud voice and their father's. But that must have been another time, Beattie wailing that she would die, just die, if she couldn't be with Jack. So she married him, after all those battles, and then she died anyway. And because of him, some might say, for how could you blame a tiny baby who barely drew breath. He married again, Beattie's Handsome Jack, and for a long time he marched in the parade once a year. Growing fatter and fatter—who would have thought? With a big red nose and his empty sleeve pinned tight.

When she was a little older Amelia sometimes went with Tom and Hugh on their jaunts about the town, and they took her to the fair once, holding both her hands. Already they were starting to become themselves, with Tom the one who worried. Would she be sick on the carousel, frightened by the Monkey Boy. Maybe not knowing that nothing could harm her while he was standing there.

Hugh didn't worry; he grew up careless, with a way of making people laugh even while they were telling him that one day he would go too far. That day at the station he made it seem like the greatest adventure, even his aunt was smiling in her musty dress, smelling like some kind of tonic. He and Tom hanging out the train window while they all blew kisses and waved their flags.

When Hugh did come back it was ten years later. She opened the door one afternoon and knew him immediately. Behind him a soft rain was falling, and when he swept off his hat in the doorway, tiny droplets scattered like a handful of flung stars. She made tea and they talked about the old house, the old days, the flu that took her parents and so many others. Her sons woke, bright-eyed and ravenous, and Hugh took off his vest and rolled around on the floor with them, Thomas and Stephen bringing out all their treasures and making a terrible mess, grinding crumbs into the carpet. While she just laughed and laughed.

Over dinner her husband asked Hugh about his work, his travels. He had been everywhere, it seemed, and was currently with a mining company in South America. Her husband knew something about engineering from his work with the city, and she drifted in and out of their technical talk, feeling light enough to float away. Thinking how strange it was that Hugh should be there, looking exactly the same. Looking even more like himself, somehow; everything a little thicker, more solid around the edges. But still with that twitching smile, the way he rubbed his thumb under his chin as he listened. The nick near the corner of his eye that was scarcely visible, even if you knew to look for it.

She wondered sometimes what her husband had thought, what he had known or seen. When he was dying for so long he forgot things, and he liked her to sit by the bed and remind him. *What did we call that dog we had, not Sadie but the other one, the one with the white tail. What was that pie you made that I used to like so much. What was the name of that fellow who came, the one who made you laugh . . .* And then he was silent, and she didn't know what he was thinking.

How long did Hugh stay—a week? A month? She had no idea, knew only that he came to see her almost every day, that she was easy in his company, in the way he knew things about her that no one else did, because they were things she would never think to mention. The doll that she carried under her right arm until she went to school, its drooping eye. The way she hid herself in the branches of trees for hours at a time, the way she wore her hair at sixteen.

Her housework suffered terribly as the weather grew warmer. They took the boys for long walks through the parks, down to the lake, and sometimes Hugh hired a car and they had picnics in the country. Once they went to see Ada, who lived in a tiny house with her younger sister. She was a little frail, a little muddled about things; she thought they had married each other and kept saying how kind they were, bringing their fine sons to visit. Telling the boys in a high, thin voice what scamps their parents had been when they were young.

Walking home, Hugh said it was all like a dream. Coming back and seeing places, people looking the same, and yet not quite. "You, for instance," he said, "you have a look of Tom, when you're serious, that I don't remember from before."

And then he told her he'd had malaria, that it came back from time to time. And he told her that once he'd seen her face in a delirium, but she didn't believe him for a minute. That kind of talk came as easily to Hugh as breathing, and didn't she used to hear them, him and Tom, lounging under the pear tree, talking about the kind of nonsense girls liked to hear. "No—no, it's true," Hugh said, and she found herself thinking.

Another time, lying on his back on a rough picnic blanket, Hugh told her what she had often wondered—that he hadn't been there when Tom died. Because she asked him, he told her some things about how it was in that place, how some men shot off feet or hands, maimed themselves in all kinds of ways, just to get out of it. Watching the clouds in the sky, he told her things so terrible she couldn't have begun to imagine them, and she knew that even these were not the worst things. Then he jumped up, roaring like a fierce tiger, and chased Thomas and Stephen over the green grass until they all fell down laughing.

Other times he talked about places he'd seen in the world, and he told her about Bolivia, where the new mine was. How the stars were much brighter there, and the moon too. The smell of the air. He described the costume he wore, riding through the hills. Baggy trousers and a wide-brimmed hat. His horse splashing through streams where native women bathed. "You should see it," he said, "you should come out there sometime."

She said that she would like to, and he said that she could come back with him, and she laughed and said of course she could, nothing to it. They joked about it after that, playing it like a game from years before. The journey by boat, by train, by cart. The house he would build and what she would see from each window. The food they would eat, the chickens and the cow in the yard. How every few months they would travel to a city, put on fine clothes and walk among the people, and how after a day they would long to be away again. They played the game over and over until she could really see herself, standing in the sunshine or riding out to meet him on a horse named Blaze.

Hugh stayed a week or a month and then he came to say good-bye, bringing presents for the boys to find when they woke. It was a warm spring night; her husband was not at home and they sat on the old swing on the back porch, drinking something cool and looking out at the dark garden. Once she thought she heard a child cry out, but upstairs her sons were fast asleep. When she turned from touching a cheek he was there in the doorway, a dark shadow glowing with light at the edges, and it was like a moment she had always known would come. He held on to her wrist very tightly as they walked back down the stairs, back through the kitchen where striped towels dried on the rack, back to the porch, the empty glasses, the swing. "Come with me," Hugh said. "You must come with me."

In the letter Hugh wrote things to hurt her, and they did hurt her. Things about life in the camp, about the dances they had at the end of the week, the makeshift lanterns and the wildness. How the women of that country, when beautiful, were very beautiful.

Around the hurtful things he wrote others. Details of his life, his work, and talk about their friendship, how much it would always mean to him. She knew Hugh, knew his boyhood swagger and the look of his back, walking away. And so she read his letters and wrote her own. Little things that were happening in the city. The birth of her third son.

She had always thought that Raymond was somehow Hugh's child. Impossible, of course, but there was a kind of life in him always, a recklessness and a careless joy that often made her catch her breath. Even the way he died—the full moon, the fast car—was so exactly what he would have chosen that in the midst of all her pain, the person she longed to tell was Hugh.

But by then the letters had stopped, and she had gotten used to that. Would have forgotten them completely, maybe, except for that way he always had of sneaking up on a person. Leaping out from behind bushes and doorways when they were children, making her scream and clasp her heart. She continued to be ambushed all her life, the brush catching in her hair as the thought of him appeared, the light catching his cheek in a certain way. Or sometimes as she never had seen him, in baggy trousers and a wide-brimmed hat, splashing through clear water.

If I am old, she thought, *then Hugh is that much older.* Or maybe dead—there was no one left who would tell her that if they happened to hear of it. No one left who would even remember that she had opened the door one afternoon and found him standing there. He could have died in an accident years ago, or from malaria or some other thing. But it seemed to her that if he had died, she would have known or remembered.

She wondered if it was the same for Hugh; she had often wondered that. It had seemed an easy decision to make at first—hardly a decision at all. Watching the daylight come into her house, the solid feel of it, of the place where she was. If she had still been that wild-haired girl, dancing through the tops of trees, it would have been a different matter. But lying in her high bed, she knew that girl was gone gone gone, drawn down long ago by the weight of the earth all around.

The next day her arms were streaked with flour and there were people coming to dinner. She watched Hugh walk away with something like relief, turning back to her own front door, and it was only later, raising a spoonful of fruit to her lips, that she began to feel the pain. To ask herself why it couldn't be true that she loved him, had always loved him, that his shadow in the doorway was the one moment it had all been leading to, and from.

So she wondered if it was the same for Hugh, or if it had been just a moment for him. A flicker of memory, the scent of lilacs in a room that was warm with the breath of sleeping children. All the things that made it impossible for her to go. People did, of course; women did. In the dark and terrible time that followed, she heard about them everywhere. In the newspaper, around dinner tables, at the grocer's counter. Ordinary women who left home and family, who gave up everything, for love. She showed herself no mercy then.

But there had been no surprise in Hugh's face when she told him, and thinking of this, she told herself that he hadn't been serious, that he knew very well the solid feel of her house, the way her sons held each hand, anchoring her to the ground. That he wouldn't have asked if he'd thought for a minute she would shake herself free and sail away beside him. She told herself this over all the things she knew, and made herself believe it. Almost believe it. An old woman still wondering—what if she had changed her mind? Had followed by the next boat, had found him on some dusty track. Would he have been delighted or appalled?

She wondered now if Hugh was the thing for her life, if there was one thing for everyone's life. A thing that kept coming around and around, a thing that stayed to the end. And then suddenly she thought that she'd gotten it all wrong; she remembered those women she'd admired in the newspaper and wondered if they'd had it mixed up too. When Hugh tightened his fingers on the base of her thumb it gave a form to things, but perhaps the real thing that took the shape of Hugh was more complex, the yearning for something else entirely. And she thought that it was such a waste, the way you started to figure things out so late. The way the knowing wasn't anything you could pass on anyway.

The way it was now, it was all coming and going. She remembered a high window, she remembered her small white bed and a time when she had longed for sleep, had longed for the dreams to start.

The thought that there was this other life going on that was hers too, but so different. Sometimes now she was aware of sinking back with just that sense of anticipation, and sometimes she wasn't aware of it at all. Sometimes she heard her name and, hearing it, realized that it had been going on for a long time, drawing her back so slowly from wherever she happened to be. Sometimes then she saw a face, almost familiar, or maybe a soft blur of pastel. And sometimes nothing but the long window, a view of tall buildings, small oblongs of sky in darkening shades. Who would choose to stay there?

That day at the fair the sky was blue and her hands were sticky, held tight by Tom and Hugh. Her heart was thumping as if it would burst, and inside her skin it was all dancing, leaping, and there was music playing, voices and wonderful hot smells. They set her on a painted horse and she held tight to the pole as it began to go up and down and around and around, and she had never been so happy. Each time around she saw Tom and Hugh watching her from the side, their arms about each other's shoulders and their caps tipped back, their smiling faces. The blue sky behind them and all the people and the wonderful hot smells and the *tap-tap* of the merry-go-round.

And then once around they weren't there, an empty space, the scuffed brown grass where they had been standing and she whipped her head around, her long hair flying and panic rising, but then they were back again and it was all right and she thought she saw Archie standing near them, his chipped tooth and his foolish freckles. She held tight to the pole and rested her cheek, the light touch on her lower lip, and there were so many people, and this time around there was someone with the look of Beattie, holding a baby and pointing, and her mother's hand with the thin gold band, tucked into the crook of her father's arm. Around and around and she thought, *What a long ride,* and she had never been so happy, going faster and faster around and around and her husband's kind eyes and Raymond with something sticky on his chin and faster and faster and Hugh laughing and all the bright stars of Bolivia and she wondered if she would go on spinning like this forever—

THE NEW WIFE

The old wife was there at the beginning. She wears her hair in an outdated style, she is trapped in her black-and-white life between the pages of a book that hasn't been opened for years. A small glossy photo with a serrated white edge, a date in black, one crumpled corner. She looks so young.

The new wife is much older, of course. They live in a house that is new to both of them, and their faces are tanned most of the year from the things they do, the places they go.

The old wife loved the beach and shook sand out of her hair on holidays. She loved to swim too, to become a tiny dot looking back at the shore. One night she swam away.

The old wife was there even before the first child, and she was the one who placed that child in his arms, all three of them touching. It was early morning; breakfast trays rattled and autumn trees blazed against a cold blue sky. He doesn't think much about the weather now, but the old wife brings it with her every time. Hot sun on the top of his head, the *clock* of the windshield wipers on a drive to the airport. The sweat between her breasts and the smell of melting asphalt through a wide-open window. For some reason he thinks of a summer night, dense and humid, filled with the sound of insects. He stands by the refrigerator, the floor almost cool beneath his feet, and the old wife sits in a circle of light at the kitchen table and that light gleams on her hair, so exactly the color of the hair of the second child, standing at her shoulder. She is astonished, the old wife, and she tells the boy she didn't know that about sea otters, tells him she thinks it wonderful that she has lived so long not knowing, while he in such a short time has come upon this fact. They are talking to each other in a circle of light, and neither one turns their gleaming head at the sound of the refrigerator door opening.

The new wife was a widow whose husband was in the same line of work; she came with her own car. He had met her a number of times over the years and he thinks of that sometimes with mild surprise, watching her put on lipstick in the little mirror in their front hall. Or when she holds his arm for balance as she reaches to untie a golf shoe. She has known him only as the successful man he is, unlike the old wife, who tied his tie before his first job interview, washed his sweat-stained shirt. Held his forehead more than once, in his youth, while he retched over a toilet bowl.

Sometimes the old wife sat in a chair by the window all day, holding a baby and watching the falling snow. Coming home in the early dark, he saw their haloed shapes and paused with one hand on the car door, something happening in his chest. There was also a time when the old wife sat by the window all day with a glass in her hand, but that was another thing entirely.

The old wife had a temper; sometimes she yelled and cried and threw things, because sometimes there were things that mattered that much. Once when he came home late he realized that he had forgotten some occasion, some event. All three of them standing facing him, winter coats and boots on, like a wall he had to break through.

The new wife has a lot to say about this and that, but she doesn't have to say it all to him. She had a life already, has hobbies and routines, a network of friends. At first he made an effort to keep them straight, to show an interest, and found that it wasn't actually much of an effort. That he was . . . not interested, maybe, but involved. She is remarkably even-tempered and hums in the mornings as she opens all the curtains. If she has moments of darkness, he has yet to see one, and even the occasional spats within her group are quickly resolved.

After the old wife swam away, he hired housekeepers, even when the children had gone. He worked hard in those years to expand his business, to spread his name, to become known as a man who got things done. And he felt like he was expanding too, as if he could be the man he was, as if he could do anything at all. He did all that and still made sure his children didn't suffer for it. He applauded at sporting events, took pictures at graduations, gave advice. As adults they seem to be neither more nor less confused or unhappy than the children of people he knows.

The old wife had the best of the children; he believes that. Oh, the sleepless nights, the mess and the worry, but also those times when only she would do. The feeling of tiny hands clasping at the back of her neck. She said once that she felt as if her job was done, but he didn't understand what she meant.

For the new wife, his children are already the people they have become, the bold outlines on a plain white ground. The man with the trim beard, the soft stomach, the red sports car. The sharp-tongued daughter whose hair is suddenly half gray. It's not surprising; she's old enough to have children of her own almost grown. But he wonders if the old wife would have gone that way too. Wonders, sometimes, what the third child would have been like.

The new wife raises funds for things, good things, and he occasionally finds himself in a straw boater and striped jacket, selling raffle tickets. She is always packing up boxes for rummage sales, and he jokes sometimes that she is giving away his old life, that what his children didn't take she is getting rid of. He jokes sometimes that she is paring them down, that she won't be satisfied until they're left with only a mat for sleeping and eating, that he never should have taken her to Japan that time. In Tokyo the new wife bought silky, shimmering things in rich colors that didn't suit her at all. They billowed when she turned before the mirror, and he wondered what she saw. The old wife would have hated the city, but she would have loved the mist on the green hills. The dainty knees of the children, walking with satchels strapped to their backs.

There is not much left of the old wife. Her name inside the front cover of a few books, a flicker in the way his children laugh or move their heads, as sudden and startling as the sting of a wasp. The book the photograph fell from was an old geometry text, and as he slots it into the box, he remembers learning that when a line is continued on into the infinite to the right, it returns again from the left. There are things that nag at him now, details he finds himself trying to recall, things the old wife would know. The name of the woman with the gap in her teeth, the color of the upholstery in their first car. The look on his daughter's face on the morning of her sixth birthday, when she opened the back door and saw the red bicycle, sunlight sparking off its spokes.

That humid night, much later, he asked the old wife what it was about sea otters. She was almost asleep. *Nothing,* she said, *it was nothing. But what,* he said, and she said it was just something the boy had read in a book. *But what,* he said, and his voice got louder because at that moment it was something he had to know. She gave a huge sigh and shifted her body; it was dark, but he could tell she wasn't looking at him. She told him that sea otters ate while floating on their backs, that they could use their stomachs as a table or as a hard surface to crack open something with a shell. That they did this, as the boy had explained, because they spent most of their life in water and hardly ever came to land.

Now you tell me, the old wife said out of the dark. *You tell me which thing came first.*

1917

In those days it was very cold and we had to wear most of our clothes at the same time, in layers, and even that was not enough. And our breath looked different when it plumed ahead of us at night, though why that should be, we had no idea. Why it should look different from our breath on a snowy night street back home, as if the air itself had altered. Perhaps just what we had come from, what we were going to. For breath is breath, isn't it, and the most important thing of all.

In those days we rode trains all over the country, and they were always cold and crowded, except when they were hot and crowded. The trains were filled with signs about the ears of the enemy, for there were supposed to be spies everywhere in those days. Often, in Paris, if we were sitting in a restaurant with someone in uniform, there would be a dapper man at the next table trying not to look like he was listening. It made us feel very strange to know someone had so much interest in our conversation. The same with the censor, and that was one reason our letters home were always cheerful; the censor would return the ones with too much truth in them. But about the trains, in those days they were always late, and they always stood still in the middle of nowhere for an hour, or two or three. So we were always hungry on trains, even if we'd brought something with us, even if we'd managed to buy a pink ticket that would get us in for breakfast or lunch. Sometimes a pack or two of cigarettes would do if we didn't have a ticket. In those days most of us learned to smoke, and there was always some prissy fellow waiting to be shocked, to say we weren't that kind of woman, were we? As if you could know anything at all about a woman from that.

In those days we were all part of the machine. It started when we stepped on the boat, waved good-bye to our family and friends, although we didn't always realize it right away. But maybe the first night, when the steward screwed the porthole closed, pulled the heavy curtain; when we tried to sleep, heads on our bulky life preservers, in a small, stuffy cabin filled with the breath of strangers. If we'd thought about it we would have assumed that someone was guiding the machine, a roomful of men somewhere, calm and in control. But the longer we were at the war, the more clearly we saw that the machine ran itself, lurching around, creating its own momentum, spitting out mangled bodies as it went.

In those days some of us were nurses and saw those bodies every day. Boys with no arms, no legs, no faces. And even if we had seen things before, factory accidents maybe, or falls from high places, we were unprepared. We changed dressings, touched hands, wrote letters that would be opened by a woman in a sunny room. Often there was a boy who was not expected to live, and we put green screens around his bed, and sometimes we sat with him, holding his hand while he struggled for breath. The noises of the ward were all around us, the squeaking wheel of a cart, the rasp of a match, the voices of the others talking and joking, or moaning, and we thought how there was no privacy in a war, not even in death.

In those days we wrote long letters home and waited and waited for word to come back from a world that was increasingly remote. We had promised to write every day, but usually we saved things up and tried to explain a week or two, forgetting things that had seemed so vital to pass on. Often we wrote in bed with our clothes on and all the covers pulled up, because in those days it was very cold. Some of us had little stoves in our rooms and we walked home with our bundles of wood to burn, like everyone else. We had brought hot-water bottles, which didn't help much, although in the mornings we could empty out the water for a wash. We wrote these things to our mothers, making it sound like an adventure, for our mothers worried about us being cold and not clean. We tried to explain how it was on Saturdays when there was hot water, and how we'd never realized that a tub of hot water could seem like the most important thing in the world. We were careful to sound cheerful, not wanting to raise eyebrows at the breakfast table, to send someone racing to the telegraph office to summon us back.

In those days it *was* all a great adventure, until the first death. Maybe the boy with the shy smile who was so polite, or the one who made us laugh out loud in the middle of a restaurant. Maybe the news came from home, a letter written from that shady street about someone we'd walked to school with every day. We wept in the dark in our cold rooms, and after that it was still an adventure, but a real one.

In those days some of us were telephone operators and some of us could speak French and were in great demand, and we all complained about the French operators, who said *Moment* and then went away forever. Everything was urgent in those days, and some of us were right up near the front lines with our tin hats and gas masks hanging on a nail and the big guns pounding, and sometimes the hut shook, sometimes we had to move out right away, and if it hadn't been such a rush we would have been very afraid.

In those days most of us cut our hair, but unlike Samson it only made us stronger. Some of us learned to drive, and sometimes we wore trousers and crawled under cars with a heavy spanner, humming "Madelon" and looking for something to fix.

In those days some of us were like Nancy and missed music most of all and we found a small piano in the back of a shop selling remnants of normal lives, and paid three boys not yet called up to hoist it four flights in the pension. We started off playing Chopin, but before long it was "Pack Up Your Troubles" and "Fancy You Fancying Me," and we all sang along until the cross woman below pounded on her ceiling with a broom or a stick and we had to stop.

In those days some of us lived in cheap hotels and some in camps, and some of us took rooms with women like Mme. Charpentier, who owned two floors in a building on rue des Lilas. Mme. Charpentier was tall with a long, thin nose; she had lost three sons and waited each day for word from two more. Their pictures were all lined up on the mantelpiece, and sometimes her lip trembled in the ticking of the clock and she touched the frames with the tip of one finger. Also living there were three elderly cousins from the country whose eyes grew moist when they talked of their beautiful château, now turned into a hospital with the grounds grown wild. The cousins sat in the salon all day, playing cards and reading the newspapers, wiping the smudges from their fingers with handkerchiefs they kept tucked in their sleeves. Mme. Charpentier always apologized for the quality of the food when we sat down to dine with the silver gleaming, even though there was only Lizette to polish it now.

In those days some of us worked in canteens in the camps, pouring coffee and hot chocolate from big pitchers, selling soap and cigarettes. We all looked like someone's mother, sister, girlfriend, and there was always someone wanting to talk to us because of that. Sometimes they talked about things they'd seen, blackened villages, rats, the pieces of a friend's body; sometimes about things they liked to do back home. Climbing the tallest tree on a dare, playing piano at parties, stealing candy when they were young, how that felt. Sometimes about dreams of the future. *Now, don't laugh,* they always said as they started. And they always said how easy it was to talk to us, how they could say things they could never tell their mothers, girlfriends, sisters. We wondered how it would be for them, going back with their heads full of things they couldn't tell a soul. Although we knew that most of them would not be going back at all.

—

In those days our feet hurt and our backs ached and we were always tired, we learned to live with that. In the evenings there was sometimes a dance, and after our long day's work we'd be in a truck, bouncing down a dark, rutted road, pulling up in front of a hut or hall packed with men. Hundreds of men and five or six of us, and we danced and a whistle blew every few minutes to change partners and sometimes there were vicious fights and we saw that too. How for the space of a dance we were not ourselves, just something everyone wanted to get their hands on. It made us feel differently about the sweet-faced boys who said we were so like their sisters, and we talked about that back in our rooms, pulling off our painful shoes, and we wondered what happened to men in groups, wondered if the war was like that.

In those days most of us fell in love, with each other or with a man in a uniform. Often it was the first time, sometimes the only one. Sometimes it ended happily but usually not. Often they were killed, and that became a small hard lump of tragedy that never went away. Sometimes we knew about the wives back home but usually not, and when we found out, we felt such fools. We were very young; it never occurred to us that people would behave that way. Some of us went too far, sneaked away on a weekend pass and met up in a station miles away, two days in a cold room with dingy curtains. If it was discovered—and it usually was, people are always moving in a war, popping up where you least expect it—we were sent home in disgrace and the shame of that was another hard thing we carried the rest of our lives.

More often in those days young men fell in love with us, especially in those canteens in the camps, the only woman with a thousand men. We pretended we didn't know, but we did, of course we did. Sometimes we used it to get things we needed, extra supplies, more wood for the fire, good behavior. It taught us things about men we were sorry to have to learn.

In those days some of us counted things. The number of steps to the Métro. The number of buttons in a jar, waiting to be sewed on. The number of times a hand grazed a human hand, doling out hot drinks. The number of coins in a pocket, the number of crosses in a field.

In those days there was often an *alerte* at night. We had to go down to the cellar, and some of us slept in our clothes because it could happen two or three times. And if we were out in the dark streets, we had to look for the blue glowing light, the closest *abri,* and hope there was room for us. Those were often the worst times, down there in the gloomy cellars, and we found ourselves noticing things strangely, and sometimes we found ourselves noticing ears and we realized that not once in our lives had we thought about ears, how individual they are. The flat, round ears of a child on his mother's lap, the big sticking-out ones of the man in the waiter's jacket. Women with long lobes or almost none, some with earrings, some without. We thought very hard about ears, waiting for the bugle to sound, but still we couldn't help thinking, *Is this how I'm going to die? Right here, with all these strangers?*

In those days some of us bought ridiculous hats.

In those days the sun did shine sometimes, and if we were in Paris we treated ourselves to lunch at Maxim's, at Prunier's. Or drank coffee at a little table outside the Café de Paris, where everyone we knew was bound to appear before the afternoon was over. Our friends were wittier than anyone we'd ever known, and we ourselves made clever jokes, something we'd never been known for. After the coffee spilled, someone wedged a matchbox under a table leg, and we laughed and laughed, and looking at the swept-clean sky, at the blaze of flowers in the market across the way, it seemed like the only place to be. But even there, at the edge of our vision, were the women and children all dressed in black.

In those days some of us went to the Gare du Nord after work to help with the refugee trains. And we didn't know what was worse, the bewildered old people or the children or the mothers with limp babies in their arms. Sometimes there would be a little boy with a blue cap, standing alone in the middle of all that noise and confusion. His hands at his stomach, clasped tightly around a carved wooden animal, a horse or a cow, maybe; it was roughly carved, and the boy only held on tighter when we asked if he would show us. And we knew that someone had carved it for him, a father or grandfather, sitting on a back step in the sun or beside the fire on a winter evening. It would have become the boy's favorite thing, he would have carried it everywhere, talked to it before he went to sleep, told it all his secrets. When we bent down to him, put an arm around his shoulders, we could feel his whole body trembling, and we walked him to the big red cross, and though we tried and tried we never found out what happened to him after that.

In those days some of us were too tired to sleep and we lay in a cold, dark room and that was when we saw our families' faces. And we thought of a day spent reading by a rain-soaked window, the tinkle of silver spoons on saucers; we tried to picture ourselves at the dinner table with our short hair and our cigarettes, our opinions. We knew that we could never go back to being dutiful daughters, and we wondered how we could ever go back at all. We thought of our innocent selves then, with great tenderness.

In those days we were all very young, although we felt older than we ever could have imagined.

In those days we never would have guessed that there would be a man with a beard and a tape recorder. That he would lean forward in a shaft of winter sunlight and say, *Do you remember anything about the war?*

EMMA'S HANDS

Emma's hands are pudgy now, but once they flailed like tiny stars; once they drifted through air like soft fronds under-water. Covered now in nicks from her sharp new teeth, from who knows what. These first tiny wounds I can't protect her from.

Emma's hands are baby hands now, generic, and it's impossible to say whose they resemble. Impossible to guess what her fingers will look like, holding a glass, touching her cheek, adorned with silver rings. But her thumbnail is my father's, broad and flat and quite distinct, appearing also in one of my sisters, another's son. It should be possible to trace that thumbnail back, to trace it like a mouth, like the shape of an eye, like a talent for music. I have tried to do it, photographs spread out on the living room floor while the day fades. While Emma sighs and whispers, lying beneath the faded blanket my mother made for me. I have tried to do it, but these ancestors keep their hands folded in laps or clenched stiffly at sides, nothing revealed. Is it the nail of Susan, who clutched the rail of the ship and saw an iceberg steal by like a nightmare? The nail of the minister with outrageous whiskers, the nail of hard-eyed Judith who waited for him to come home? The nail of the lawyer who lost his wife, the nail of the grocer who whipped his sons, the nail of the son dead in a French field? Is it the nail of William, who gripped a pen between strong fingers, who dipped and wrote, scratching the page, faster and more furiously? Or does it belong to his wife, who opened that letter miles away? The hands of Norah, who folded the letter, who folded all the letters, and kept them together in a place where they would be safe for over a hundred years.

There is a photograph of Norah, middle-aged. Taken against the wall of a house, head and shoulders, enlarged, with a misty blur where the arms should be, cropped before the hands, which are surely lying clasped in her lap. She might be smiling; her lips are almost smiling, but there is something about the eyes. . . .

She looks astonishingly like her youngest child, my grandmother, as I knew her. But at the time of the letters my grandmother was not even a thought, a speck of a possibility. At the time of the letters there were only the two small boys, and a black hole where Clara had been.

Norah traveled home by boat and train, a journey that could take three days, a journey that would give her too much time to think. It was August, hot in her layers of black, but there would have been a breeze on the deck of the boat and perhaps she walked there, perhaps she gripped the rail like her great-grandmother, also looking into the vast unknown. She would have prayed; she might have thought of jumping.

—

She had met him after church one day. He had come to visit a distant relative, being in need of a complete change of scene. Or so he told her later in the week, when they went out walking in a brisk spring wind. He told her other things, told her about his successful business, the small house in the booming town near the lake. And then he astonished her by suddenly leaping straight into the air to pluck a blossom from an overhanging branch. He landed awkwardly, almost falling, and even while she clapped a hand to her lips, she noticed how he somehow maintained his serious air as he stumbled, as he straightened and with a small bow offered her the flower. In the same way he asked if he might write to her when he returned home, and pressed her hand for a moment when they parted.

"This is the story," my grandmother said, "of how my father met my mother."

"Listen," my grandmother said, "because I am the last one, there is no one else who can tell you these things.

"Listen," my grandmother said, and I listened. But I also examined my fingernails, scratched my knee. Thought of the boy with brown eyes who had smiled at me the day before. The tiny apartment was hot, crammed with several lifetimes of furniture, of china. Summer treetops, not moving, through the balcony doors.

"Listen," my grandmother said, and I thought I did. But now that I have come to this time that she thought of, this time when I would want to know, I find that I have only scraps, and I wonder if it is enough. And I wonder if she also made her story from bits and pieces, if her mother did, and hers before.

—

He must have written to her when he returned home, but she didn't keep those letters. Sitting at his cluttered desk at the back of the store, or late at night in his tidy house he would have told her more about himself, his prospects. He had already decided that they should be married soon after her nineteenth birthday, if she consented. He had arranged to come back at Christmas to speak with her father, and suggested that the ceremony be performed then, to save the trouble and expense of another long journey.

"Oh, love," her aunt Fan said when she asked the question. "That will come, don't you fret about that."

So he came at Christmas, and she had thought him taller. They traveled back together, the longest journey she had ever taken, and moved into the small house in the busy town, and it was not so different, really, from keeping house for her father. When Clara was born she thought she knew what Aunt Fan had meant. Holding Clara in her arms, the bright eyes and tiny mouth, head bobbing on her fragile neck like a small bird in search of food. She lived in a long swoon then, overwhelmed. It was similar with the others when they were babies, but never the same. Looking at Clara, she saw the best of herself, and her husband, and all who had gone before.

When Clara was three, William bought a second house, a rambling old place by the lake. In the summers Norah stayed there with the children and her housemaid, Edie, and he came on Saturdays, after the store had closed. The days were long and lazy, and even though there must have been more work to do with only Edie to help, it never seemed that way. They ate all their meals together in the kitchen, because it was easier, and sometimes they laughed until their sides ached. Often in the mornings she would leave Edie to watch the boys and would walk along the beach with Clara, who was now almost seven. There were other houses along the lake, and there must have been other people, but it seemed that she never saw anyone, heard anyone. Just the shrieks of James and Arthur fading into the sighing of the water while she and Clara walked as far as the big dead tree, pausing, bending down whenever a glittering stone caught their eye.

Summer, then, at the house by the lake, the beach house where curtains blow at the open windows in a faded photograph. The trellised veranda where the sisters are captured, grown, taking tea in long dresses, leaning back in cane chairs. If Clara had lived, she would have been one of those sisters. Married, for they all married, had children. Widowed by a war or disease, she would have learned to drive, gone to church, worn gloves when she left the house. Lived long enough to complain that the world had changed, and not for the better.

But the sisters who sip tea on the shady veranda never knew Clara, had not even a wisp of a memory. Their oldest brothers may have, although they were young and blinkered by their own world— the sand, the lake like a vast sea. But she may have visited them in dreams all their lives; it may have been Clara who made the covers twitch.

Norah left the boat at Prescott, lay awake all night at the Daniels Hotel, and boarded the train in the morning. The carriage rocked and she almost slept, and dreamed or remembered the night before Clara took sick. Sitting in the old rocker on the veranda as she did every night when the children were asleep, the mending done. It was Friday, late, and she could hear Edie moving about the kitchen, preparing food for the next day. She looked forward to William's arrival, of course she did, but there was always a moment when she realized that the man she missed was not quite the one who came stepping down the dusty road. She smiled, though, at the way the children ran to him as he mounted the steps, searched his pockets for the cubes of sugar he brought them from the store. And she smiled after breakfast when he lined them up, saying he was a general inspecting his troops. The way Arthur, who was three, tried to make himself taller, the way they all kept their eyes straight ahead while their father pretended to adjust a medal, squint down a gun barrel. It was just that his voice was too deep, somehow, rumbling through the house; his hand on her shoulder too heavy when it was time to climb the stairs.

The train rocked, and she dreamed or remembered the veranda at night, the sleepy sound of insects. She heard Edie creak up the back stairs to bed, she watched the moon rise and sometime later heard a tiny noise, looked to see Clara standing barefoot in the open doorway.

"I couldn't find you," Clara said, only half awake, "but I knew you must be somewhere, so I just kept looking."

Norah took Clara on her lap like a much smaller child, and they rocked and talked about the moon, and she smelled the faded sun in her hair.

Her father met her at the station; he moved toward her, but only to pick up her bags. With the reins between his hands he told her how sorry he was, and asked about the journey. When they pulled up in front of the house, Aunt Fan appeared and bustled her off to bed, brought her a cup of tea and closed the door quietly as she left. The milk formed a skin in the cup as she lay in her old bed, knowing that it was a mistake to be there but wondering where else she could have gone.

It all happened so quickly. The pain that got worse, and the fever. On Sunday she asked William to go for the doctor, but he said what he had so often said, in company, at the dinner table. That he wouldn't have one in the house. That they were quite capable of looking after their own. He sat with Clara himself all afternoon, squeezing out cloths to lay on her burning forehead, spooning broth that she couldn't keep down.

In the evening her eyes were still blazing, and they bathed her again in cool water and dried her very gently, and she did seem a little better, just whimpering now, and tired. Norah sat up through the night in a hard chair, talking and sometimes singing softly, rising only to place another cloth on Clara's head, sponge her face and neck, the water dripping loudly back into the blue china bowl. She must have slept, for she woke suddenly with the sound of seabirds, and her first thought was that the worst was over and Clara was sleeping peacefully. But then she knew, and nothing she had ever heard or seen or thought had prepared her for that moment.

People began to call the day after she arrived. The pastor first, the women of the village who had known her all her life. Most of them had lost children, most had lost more than one, and they patted her hand and told her that it would hurt less with time. She didn't believe them; she thought she could still see the shadows in their eyes, in the corners of their mouths.

The pastor talked about Clara being in a better place. *The little angel,* he kept calling her.

But she wasn't, Norah wanted to say. Didn't say. She wasn't a little angel, not that. She had a wild temper when she thought things weren't fair, and she wasn't afraid of anything except the dark in the middle of the night, and that not always. She would have been a fighter, Norah wanted to say, although she wasn't sure what she meant by that.

"I should have gone myself," Norah said.

Aunt Fan had grown deaf; she had to say it louder, again and again.

"For the doctor. When William wouldn't. I should have gone myself."

The words seemed to hang, jagged, just before her eyes. It was an early cold but the stove kept the big kitchen warm. Through the window the trees were just beginning to flame, and when Aunt Fan rubbed her hands together, flour danced in the air.

"Oh, doctors," she said. "It might not have made any difference at all. Your William is a clever man. Chances are the doctor wouldn't have helped at all."

She went back to her kneading, and Norah worked the fringe of her shawl. She didn't remember much about it, but she did remember William's face. When he appeared in the doorway, pushing at his collar stud, his mind already on the busy week ahead. When he saw them lying there in Clara's narrow bed. He was a clever man, her William, but she saw in his face that he had been wrong. He knew what was best, William did, but he hadn't known that Clara would die, and with her arms around her child, she saw his face splinter, fall apart, and that was when she howled.

—

The photograph of William is familiar: he looks like all those fathers and sons who appear in cardboard boxes at auctions, at flea markets. Tight collar, carefully combed hair, thin mouth. It is difficult to imagine him hiding lumps of sugar in his pockets for the children to find, difficult to imagine him laughing. Is that just the fault of photography? A serious business, after all. Trips to the studio, holding a pose. There are no blurred shots of William throwing a ball to his sons or walking barefoot in the cold lake, but it is quite likely that he did those things. Just as it is likely that he also felt pain, and grief, and confusion.

And it may not be fair to blame William for his inheritance: his father's stern whiskers above the surplice, his mother's black bonnet. Not fair to blame William for the state of medicine. A ruptured appendix still not a simple thing, and as Aunt Fan said, the doctor may not have made any difference. It is not even fair to blame William for not keeping Norah's letters; there may not have been any to keep. His own are filled with complaints of her silence. Bewilderment, impatience, and finally anger at her prolonged absence.

The letters began to arrive two days after she did. *My own dear wife,* they all began.

Norah read them in her old room, in the pale light that washed through the window. She read each one once, when it arrived, and then put it in a wooden box that had belonged to her mother. After she had snapped the lid shut she lay back on her high bed, watching the shadows of leaves on the ceiling and wondering what it was that she felt.

You must take care of yourself, William wrote. *Eat well and rest and come home soon. And above all avoid the drafts in that old house.*

The boys are well behaved and Mother is managing fine, William wrote, *although she finds Edie rather lax. I have yet to receive a letter from you, and hope that the morning's post will bring me some word. You must not brood, Norah, although I confess that I do not know what else you will be able to do there.*

The boys miss you terribly, William wrote, *and ask when you are coming home.*

She stopped to wonder about that. She loved her sons, but from the moment they left her arms they began to move away from her, marching down the dusty beach road behind their father.

Still no word from you, William wrote, *and I can only wonder at your coldheartedness. I know that you grieve, as I do, but you have other children, and a husband, and it is not right that you should abandon us in this way.*

It is now six weeks, William wrote, *and you have been away long enough. If you take the morning train on Wednesday next you can be on the first boat, and I will be there to meet you Friday at three. I am enclosing enough money for the fare from the dock, should you get this letter sooner and wish to leave on Monday. I cannot imagine what you are doing all this time.*

The minister pressed her hand; his was very cool, and she remembered Clara's cheek.

"You must not fall into despair," he said, and the word tolled through her head for days.

Her father spoke of the benefits of fresh air and exercise, and she listened. She tried to go out walking but felt herself too sharply drawn, a harsh black figure in the landscape, her voice too rough and her hands thick and unwieldy. Within the house she knew this was not true; her rings slipped loose on her fingers, and Aunt Fan was always coaxing her to eat. Within the house she seemed to have no shape at all, she was like a shadow falling on an armchair, crossing a threshold. And, like a shadow, making no real mark. Her father read in the evenings, Aunt Fan sewed beneath the lamp, and sometimes Norah helped her. And sometimes her heart caught, watching her hands in the soft folds of an old shirt, the needle clenched tight between thumb and finger, and she felt she was on the edge of knowing something, taking hold of something. She saw William in the doorway, as she had seen him. His fingers frozen on the collar stud, his face suddenly splintered, naked. In the split second before she howled, she had almost heard a tiny *click,* as if a door had opened somewhere. Opened a crack, just enough to know it was there. Clutching a needle in her father's house, she thought about the door and knew all at once that she would not go through it.

Clara would have, she thought. *Clara was never afraid of an open door.* But as the clock began to tick again, she wasn't sure if even that was true.

She went back, of course. Traveling by train and boat, the same journey in reverse. It would have been colder, but she may have stood on the deck anyway, gripped the rail, as she watched William grow larger and larger at the end of the pier.

She went back to the small house in town and to the big house by the lake and she had nine more children, boys and girls. And she died not long after someone photographed her against the wall of the beach house, looking like my grandmother, who was her last born. She died three years before Arthur was scattered in France, four years before William slumped over the counter in the store, six years before Bea coughed for the last time. Years before James was arrested, before Samuel beat his wife, before Janet began to drink. But perhaps not long before the picture of her daughters taking tea on the veranda. The four sisters who all married doctors and became the source of many gentle jokes.

And perhaps it is not her hand at all, this hand Emma wraps around my baby finger. Perhaps it never was. But there is another photograph, one that I do not have. In it too it is impossible to see Norah's hands. She faces her child, and Clara looks up. The background is a hazy wash of sun, and the fingers of her left hand are buried in the tangles of Clara's long curls, which must be warm to the touch. They are looking at each other. They are smiling.

DOWN
BY THE LAKE

~~~~~~

Down by the lake, Jess says, "I've been thinking about that yellow mixing bowl," and Babe says, "Uh-huh." Then she waits while Jess gives her purse a shake, listening for the chink of the car keys. Jess does this every so often as they walk, but it's not because she's old. Her whole life, she's had the feeling she could easily misplace something important.

"Just look at that," she says, and Babe knows she's talking about the sight of her bare foot on the hard sand. Its paleness and the thickened nails and the cords and bumps all over the place. It looks an alien thing, although the sad truth is that it fits right in with the way the rest of their bodies look now, getting ready for bed at night.

"Remember Miss Earnshaw?" Babe says, and Jess says, "Uh-huh." On a Sunday-school excursion to Kincardine once. Miss Earnshaw grew up in China, became a missionary like her parents. Her face was very wrinkled and a strange yellowish shade—from living there so long, everyone supposed. On the beach she sat down on a flat rock and took off her shoes and stockings to shake out the sand. She was missing two toes on her right foot.

On the way home the motion of the train sent them all to sleep, and when Babe opened her eyes, Miss Earnshaw was shaking her shoulder, her yellow face so close Babe could see something wet and glistening in the deep folds that ran down from the corners of her mouth. Babe screamed; she couldn't help it. After that they scared each other at night, going up the long dark stairs. Hauling on the banister and thumping their feet unevenly, each pretending to be Miss Earnshaw coming to get the other.

Although it's still August, the air is getting cooler down by the lake as the sun begins to fade. It's one of those evenings when the water is flat and still, a soft greenish-gray like a dress Babe had once, and sound carries a long way. They can hear people setting tables in the cottages they walk by, and mothers telling children to wash their hands right now. At one place they pass a girl turning cartwheels in a circle on the cool sand; she doesn't even look at them.

"How old was Catherine?" Jess says, although she knows very well. "Nine," Babe says, knowing that Jess knows, that the question is just a way to start them thinking. They've lived together so long that it needs only a word or phrase, sometimes even a look; they don't actually talk much, but their shared thoughts are a conversation that goes on all the time.

This year there's a tree trunk that's washed up from somewhere, lying across the beach past the last cottage. Not a trunk, a whole tree, really, but it's been worn so silvery smooth that it's all of a piece, the web of branches and the tufted base where the fine roots would have been. The way it lies, it's just the right height, and they lower themselves carefully. Jess reaches into her bag, jingling the keys, and brings out the battered cigarette case that belonged to their brother Roy. It was sent back from France with the rest of his things, and for a long time it sat on a table in the front room with his badges and the picture he'd sent them, looking serious in his uniform and cap. Their mother was death on smoking and drinking, all that kind of thing. Where would he get something like that cigarette case, she kept saying after she'd opened the package. They all knew it was from Adele, but they didn't say a word. All five of them watching as he packed things the night before he left. *Now, don't tell Mother,* Roy said, showing them; *you know how she is.* They all promised and none of them ever did tell.

Roy had tucked the shiny cigarette case in with his thick socks, and his shadow was huge as he walked back and forth in the lamplight, and he had to duck every time he came near the point where the roof sloped over the head of his bed. Willie and Tom and Art dragged the heavy bag downstairs, stumbling over one another, and Roy came staggering after, carrying Jess and Babe on each arm as they liked him to do, even though they were far too heavy. Their arms touched around his neck.

"I wonder what they said to each other," Jess says, thinking about their father with the wagon hitched up, white mist pluming from the horses' nostrils, waiting to drive Roy to meet the late train. Their father thought Roy was a fool to go when he was needed on the farm, and when they got the news, he said, *Dammit, I told him,* over and over, and their mother didn't say a word though she was death on swearing too.

When the cigarette case came back it was scratched and chipped and dented, and they thought that was from bullets and battles. For a while they thought it their duty to give it back to Adele, somehow, but then their mother came back from town one day and said she'd actually seen her laughing, walking down the street, so they knew she didn't deserve it. It must have gone to one of the boys later, then made its way back to Babe and Jess. They are the last ones left, and a lot of things have come back to them in cardboard boxes or old suitcases.

The tree trunk is already cooling in the evening air; they can feel it through the faded plaid wool trousers they wear. They sit puffing on their cigarettes, looking out through the clouds of tiny black flying things that hover near the water's edge. Farther down, a boat roars out from the shore, cutting a path that takes a long time to heal.

"Poor Mother," Jess says.

It wasn't fair, the way it took her near the end. The way she'd throw off all her clothes and start to wander off downtown if you weren't watching her every minute. Some days there was nothing to be done but tie her in a chair. They never knew much about her early life, or they might have been able to make some sense of the things she said. Calling out names that weren't familiar to them, calling someone to bring a bucket, to catch that damn dog, to hush now, hush now. Sometimes she patted her knee, gingerly, as if she'd fallen down and scraped it. And sometimes she'd croon *Jenny Jenny Jenny*, over and over again. That was her own name.

They were already living in town then, in the old house Willie bought cheap after Mr. Warren hanged himself. Willie kept saying he was going to get married and fill it with children, but he never did. None of them had children, unless maybe Art did and no one thought to tell them. Art went out West on a harvest excursion and never came back. Sent them a card when he got married, and once in a while after. Then a letter from his wife came to say he'd died in an accident. She'd signed her full name, as if just Eleanor was too informal.

Certainly Tom never had any children, living out on the farm, getting stranger and stranger. Selling off the front field for those Boyds to fill up with wrecked cars.

"What a blessing Father didn't live to see that," Jess says.

For a while Tom was a bootlegger; Babe heard talk when she taught in the high school. A big belly and an old undershirt, tufts of gray hair growing down the back of his neck. That was the same Tom whose eyes glowed in the lamplight in Roy's room, who came running through the door yelling about Catherine falling, about the blood.

"Poor Mother," Jess says again, and Babe says, "Uh-huh."

"I don't remember any hugs or kisses, any dears or darlings," Jess says, "do you?"

She asks because Babe is almost two years older, because Jess is never quite sure she didn't miss out on something, forget something.

"No," says Babe. "But that wasn't her way, was it? She was good to us though, never hit us, like some."

"Just the once," Jess says, and Babe says, "Uh-huh."

On their way out of town to the lake they have to pass by the old farm, the place where it used to be.

"We could have been sitting pretty," Babe always says, looking over. Jess keeps her eyes on the road and the red needle on the speedometer. When Tom died, they found out that the bank owned the farm; they never figured out what he did with the money. The last people who bought it tore down the old house, the barn, and made Amber Acres. Lot after lot, house after house, stretching all the way back to the bluff overlooking the lake.

In the old days it was all bush back behind, but there was a rough sort of road or path. You came through it and suddenly, what you never expected. The cry of gulls and crashing waves and water stretching as far as you could see. Babe said it was Michigan on the other side, far—even farther than the horizon. She knew things like that when they were children. Babe went to high school, then on to the Normal. She taught in a country school first, where the big boys who came in the winter chewed up wads of paper and flicked them off their rulers all over the room. Then she taught geography in the high school for so long that her classes were filled with children of the children she'd taught.

They'd always said Jess had a weak heart, something that made the new young doctor laugh when she went to see him. *Sound as a bell,* he said, *you'll outlive me*—although she could tell by his curly sideburns, his mustache, and his bright green shirt that he didn't really think that. But sound as a bell anyway, so she could have gone to high school after all, and then on to who knew what. A five-mile walk it was, there and back, and the first two days she was so tired she fell asleep at the supper table, fell right off her chair. But she was desperate to go, to keep going, and when they said it was too far, too hard with her weak heart, she begged her father to drive her in, but he refused. *Plenty to do right here,* he said, and her mother agreed. It was a shame, she was smart as a whip, everybody said. She read everything she could get hold of, and Babe shared everything she could, but it wasn't the same, she knew that. It was something she always felt the lack of, in company, in conversation. Something she got used to.

"Maybe they were just scared of losing you too," Babe says, and Jess shrugs.

"Those mornings I had to get up in the dark," Babe says. "Or when I boarded with that old couple out near Brussels."

"The place with the cornhusk tick?" Jess says, and Babe says, "Uh-huh. Don't believe I slept a wink that whole year. I'd lie there in the middle of the night with those lumps and bumps poking into me, thinking about that feather tick we had at home. Then thinking about all of you there in the house, sleeping and dreaming in the dark. Made me cry and cry, and I was that envious of you, Jess, not having to go out in the world like me."

"Uh-huh," Jess says; she's heard it before.

The sun is moving now, and the sky is starting to take on color—orange and mauve, a rich pale blue. They push themselves up from the log, holding on to each other until they get their balance and start to walk back to where they've parked the car, shoes sitting neatly on the front seat with the socks tucked inside.

"Those mornings he used to take you to meet the early train," Jess says, "when you were at the Normal. What did you talk about?"

They have reached a small, stony patch and pick their way carefully before Babe answers.

"I don't know at all," she says. "I can't remember a thing, do you know, I can't remember a thing he might ever have said."

There was a story about Catherine as a baby; he must have told that. One night she wouldn't settle and their mother was exhausted, at her wit's end. He carried Catherine downstairs in his stocking feet, stoked up the fire and sat holding her, watching it. She quieted, watching the flames, and after a while she fell asleep on his chest and he sat there while the fire died, his nose so cold and his breath starting to show, afraid to move a muscle lest he wake her.

Catherine and Roy were the oldest, and even though there wasn't much more than a year between any of them, it seemed like it must have been different. Like they were born to two different people, born out of something that couldn't help but be soon used up. Otherwise it was impossible to imagine.

The lake stretches away, vast beside them, and it's easy to understand how some first white man would have thought he'd reached the ocean. The bafflement when he found the water fresh.

"Well, you can only make the world from what you know," Babe says. "Build it up piece by piece from the things you believe to be true."

After their mother died, things were getting more expensive, and they let out a room, the one at the top of the back stairs. The first time to the teacher who'd taken Babe's place at the high school, but it didn't work out. Strange noises and creaking stairs and one night Jess met the Durant boy putting on his shoes in the moonlit kitchen. After the teacher, there was a clerk from the bank who blinked very fast when anyone spoke to him. He was quiet enough, but one night he set the bedclothes on fire, didn't even wake up until Babe dumped a bucket of water over everything. Then Margaret Hatch from the grocery, who was no trouble at all.

Now they keep the upstairs closed off, to save on the heat and the stairs. They go up in the spring to dust and sweep, but that's about all. In the top drawer of a dresser up there is an old envelope full of hair. Seven chunks of hair, each one tied with a bit of white ribbon, looking much the same. As if it didn't matter who they belonged to, but Jess wonders suddenly if her mother always knew. If she didn't need to distinguish because she just knew. She doesn't like it, but she can't help thinking sometimes that maybe there's another side to everything she knows. That maybe hardness is sorrow. That a stony silence enfolds all the tenderness in the world.

It's getting dark as they drive slowly down the highway. They can't see the lake from where they are, but the colored sky marks it for them. When they pass Amber Acres, Babe doesn't say anything about the view. Instead what she says is "Will you still go down there?"

"Oh, I don't know," Jess says. "Maybe not."

So far they've all died in order, sisters and brothers, and if what they told Babe at the medical center is true, they still will. As they round the bend and start down the hill, the lights of the town are spread out below them, and it looks quite grand and full of promise.

"Home again home again," Jess says, like always, and Babe says, "Uh-huh."

And then she says, "We were just young, we didn't know any better."

"That's so," Jess says.

It doesn't seem possible that it was the same day, but that's how they remember it. Bitter cold and everything covered with ice, the branches of trees through the window like something out of a storybook, diamonds and daggers. The sharp-edged frozen ruts of the lane. Their mother in her bluish apron standing, stirring. Babe and Jess on chairs, their chins resting on the kitchen table, staring at the yellow mixing bowl; she is making a cake and has promised them that if they wait very still and quiet, they can lick out the bowl. Willie watching out the window, the big black winter window, watching for the older ones coming up the lane, home from school. Then suddenly the yelling, Tom shrieking about blood, about Catherine falling and Roy staggering, trying to carry her, their father running to meet them, slipping and sliding. Catherine's white, frozen face on the kitchen floor and all that blood from her head.

For some reason Babe and Jess are alone in the kitchen, and they dip a finger into the batter in the yellow bowl, and once they start they can't stop, it's the best thing they've ever tasted, and then they're scooping it up in their small hands and it's running everywhere, between their fingers, over their chins. Their mother comes through a door and she says something or maybe nothing at all, and she grabs the wooden spoon from the bowl, batter flies everywhere, on the cupboard, on the wall, and she hits and hits and hits them until the wooden spoon breaks in two.

SPANISH GRAMMAR

Franco has been dead for a year, and the signs are everywhere. On the sooty sides of buildings and bus shelters, curved around the bumpers of small cars. Even through the café window she sees them, nailed to the trunks of old trees. *Democracia—Sí! Vote Sí!* And here and there a succinct black *No*. If she closes her eyes alternately, she can make them appear, disappear.

Sí—no—sí—no.

Stay. Go.

Jaime explained the referendum once, in a noisy underground bar. "It's a farce," he said, "there has been no education. How can the people make a choice when they don't even understand the question?"

"Pay attention," Manolo said from the other side of the table. "He's right for once, listen to what he says."

Jaime talks over laughter and crashing glasses, and she leans toward his voice; she knows that some kind of history is going on, and she really does want to understand. But while she listens, she also watches the way his lips move, forming each word, the way his fingers curve around a squat glass of wine. And she knows that when she tries to remember the conversation, later, these will be the things that have stayed with her.

Manolo is Jaime's roommate; he studies geography at the university when he is not handing out leaflets on street corners, marching in forbidden places. They never know when he will come slamming through the door, smudges on his face, bruises on his elbows. Bringing them stories of miraculous escapes, racing down alleys, crawling under parked cars. "It's a wonderful time to be alive," he says. "Possibilities are suddenly in the air. You can almost touch them, taste them."

He bounces on the edge of the rumpled bed, waving his arms and laughing while Jaime, embarrassed, goes to make coffee.

"You should have seen it," he says to her. "Ay, Jaime," he calls, "you should have been there."

There is a raw scrape above his right eyebrow and cold air rises from his heavy sweater, a faint, smoky smell.

Manolo likes to talk English with her; he claims to have learned it all from old Beatles records.

"I am the walrus," he says solemnly. "A very useful phrase."

At one time she thought that Jaime might be jealous of Manolo's quick, slangy English, the way she and Manolo laugh and laugh together. A certain tension in Jaime when he appears in the doorway, carrying three cups on a plastic tray.

"Manolo is my friend," he says later, when she tries to talk about it. Smooth it.

"Don't you understand anything," he says, with an anger in his voice that she has not heard before.

"I'm sorry," she whispers, trying to see his face in the dark. "I only meant . . ."

"Don't say it to me," he says. "Manolo is the one you have insulted. Don't you know anything?"

Some subtle code of honor that she has crashed right into with her clumsy American feet.

"Canadian," she says automatically. She falls asleep thinking how silly it is, this argument they are having in loud whispers, in a foreign language.

Jaime claims not to speak English at all, but she knows that is not true. She remembers his accent, the first words he spoke to her.

"It doesn't matter," he says. "The point is that if I were in America—okay, in Canada—I would be speaking English. No? And you are in my country now."

She agrees with him in principle. But it means that she is the one who becomes tangled and lost in the space between words. Shades of meaning.

She closes her eyes.

In her favorite café, the young waiter brings another cup of coffee, reaches to empty the ashtray again. His name is Javier and he has a cousin in Canada; in Montreal, he says, or maybe Vancouver. The cousin writes that it is always cold and that the people are the color of newspaper.

"Is it true," Javier says, "that Canada is covered with snow and ice, that the sun disappears for half the year?"

He doesn't seem to believe her answer, asks the same thing each time he sees her, as if hoping she'll let the truth slip out.

The café is owned by Javier's uncle, who is not really his uncle but a good friend of his father. The tables lean and the floor is scattered with bits of paper, cigarettes, but it is nearly empty in the afternoons, and if the uncle's back is turned, Javier sometimes brings her a free cup of coffee, a small glass of brandy. He is almost fourteen and already an outrageous flatterer, praising her accent, her vocabulary, her eyes. He can't believe that she learned it all in school, says that he, for example, didn't learn a single thing when he used to go to school.

Between customers Javier washes dishes behind the counter, watching himself in the misty mirror that also reflects the leaning tables, the door. Takes out a white comb and passes it through his hair, smoothing the wake with his left hand. There is a tight swagger in his walk that tells her in another year or two he will be unbearable, lounging around fountains, clicking his tongue, calling out after all the girls. But in the meantime he is almost fourteen and amazed by his own reflection. Still wanting to hear about a place where people live beneath the snow, at the dark end of the world.

The café table is scattered with books and papers. A map of the city and a blue pad with a rising airplane on the cover. Two postcards, a newspaper, a thick red notebook and a text of Spanish grammar. She has been trying to write a letter, but the pen lies abandoned across a flimsy blue page. *Still here,* it says, *although the weather's getting colder.* And something about the rain, how it drips down through the wet yellow trees in all the parks in the city.

In the first weeks she was determined to do it right. She left the apartment early, collected maps and guidebooks and walked the crisp blue city for hours. Plaza Mayor, Plaza Canovas, Puerta del Sol. She bought the textbook, notebook, a black pen, and produced new phrases for Jaime in the evenings. He was pleased but mostly amused.

"I thought you were on holiday," he said, "what are you doing working so hard?

"Come over here," he said, "you speak well enough already."

Translate into Spanish: What do you want?
Translate into English: Es necesario comprender todo.

She still goes out each day, though not so early. Walks through twisting familiar streets until she reaches the Gran Via. Walks through the park, around and around, stopping by the gray waters of the artificial lake. When it rains, she follows tour groups in the Prado, sits on a wooden bench in front of a dark painting of a royal family. Some days she spends hours in the café across from the park, completing exercises, copying sentences in the red notebook. The things she reads often astound her. Past Contrary-to-Fact Conditions. Present Unreal Conditions. The significance of the subjunctive mood.

Translate: Tengo hambre. Tengo frío. Tengo dolor.
    I am hungry. I am cold. I have pain.

"What did you do today," Jaime says as the streetlights flicker on. Sometimes she says, "Waited for you," because sometimes it is true. But she always laughs when she says it, giving him a choice.

—

In the Spanish language the verb "esperar" means both to wait and to hope: meaning must therefore be determined by context.

She meets Jaime near his office in the evenings, and they make their way through crowded streets, through brightly lit bars thick with cigarette smoke and laughter. Wine in heavy tumblers and long glass cases displaying mysterious foods. Something that looks like kite string wrapped around a cross of wood.

"What is that," she says, and when she doesn't recognize the word, Jaime points to his stomach, making signs.

"*Intestines?*" she says, and he laughs at her squeamishness.

"Try this," he says, touching different delicacies to her lips.

"Open," he says, "open."

And she does.

Often Manolo is with them at the beginning of the evening. On his way to a meeting, to paint signs, or, more rarely, to study. They are always in motion, sampling tapas here and there, a meal somewhere else, coffee. Meeting Jaime's friends everywhere, in bars and restaurants, in front of shopwindows. Everyone wants to touch him; the men slap his back, punch his shoulder, and the women rest their hands on his as he bends to light their cigarettes. She sees now how rare it was in the summer. Lying on a beach in the south with their little fingers resting side by side.

"We don't have to go out every night," she says. "You don't have to entertain me."

But he says, "It's the way I live. Whether you are here or not."

It seems to be true; his apartment is clean and bare, a place to shower and sleep, occasionally make coffee. If Manolo is home, they never make love.

"Very quietly," she whispers, but he whispers that it wouldn't be polite. He would prefer to live alone, if only he could afford it. Most of his money goes to Barcelona, to his wife and son.

"Divorce is not so easy," he says. "Anyway, my son would still be my son.

"You Americans," he says, stroking her cheek. "Is that all you're after?"

She has asked herself that, sitting on a bench in the Prado, not looking at a picture of a royal family. Thought about how she reads his skin with her fingertips, memorizing clauses, parentheses. Thought about how she watches his profile, driving in the car, how something about it twists right to her heart. There is some secret in the hollow of his temple, the tiny scar near the corner of his eye. Some explanation in the sweep of his lashes that she can't catch hold of, though sometimes it skewers right to her heart.

They go away most weekends, driving and driving to all the places he wants to show her. Toledo, Segovia, San Sebastian. Listening to a tape she bought for him, Bob Dylan singing about simple twists of fate. Or sometimes his own favorite, wild guitar rising. He raps his thumb on the steering wheel and cries out with Paco de Lucia, *Ay, mi alma.* My soul, my soul.

"There's a concert next month," he says. "I'll take you, would you like that?

"If you are still here," he says.

"If I am still here," she says.

—

Translate: It is important to know the rules.

It has always been this way. In darkened rooms they praise each other extravagantly, but in daylight they assume little. Like that from the beginning, though perhaps not so obvious. Chance meeting by the sea, in summer. She remembers the sand beneath her bare feet, the weight of the oranges she carried in a paper sack. Moonlight, later, and the soft scent of flowers.

The past (or imperfect) tense is the most regular and the easiest to form of all the tenses.

The arrangement allows them to be very kind to each other. They exchange childhoods, produce small treasures from pockets when they meet in the evening.

"What would you like to do," Jaime says, "we'll go anywhere, do anything you like. I only want you to be happy."

And she believes him. But sometimes at night he makes soft blowing noises in his sleep, and she nudges him with an elbow, hard, harder, until he stops. And sometimes it frightens her, how she hits him when he is sleeping, as hard as she can.

Often she knows she made a mistake, following him into real life. Following him a week later, hitching from the south in a straight line, his address on a scrap of paper, growing creased and warm in her clenched hand. Her fingers tremble, she can barely dial the telephone, yet she hears her own voice, casual, saying, "Well. Hello. Just passing through."

But she also remembers that he left his office right away. That he found her in a crowded bar, that he couldn't stop smiling, shaking his head and smiling. These are the things she balances against the apartment where her clothes stay piled on a chair by the door, the women who touch his hands as he bends to light their cigarettes. The look on his face, scanning the room for her. The way he stops and hugs her in the middle of a crowded street, and the way he says her name sometimes.

Jaime's apartment is small and bare and her clothes stay piled by the door on an old wooden armchair that his wife bought, the first year of their marriage. She is not allowed to answer the telephone; he says that people are following Manolo, that she may be tricked into giving something away. She finds it hard to believe that anyone could think Manolo dangerous, but they both have stories of friends who have been arrested, jailed. One who was shot while disputing a parking ticket.

Some mornings the telephone wakes her, ringing and ringing. She imagines the secret police, blue-jawed and steely-eyed, hunched over the receiver at the other end. Or, more often, Jaime's wife clutching a cigarette between red-tipped fingers, blowing angry puffs of smoke while the telephone rings. Part of the reason she walks the city all day, although the main part is that she doesn't want him to think she sits in a chair by a window, waiting for him.

They go away most weekends, driving and driving, and all the places Jaime shows delight her. She is amazed at how he knows his country, knows where to find a tiny, perfect church in a town with dusty streets, knows where to eat chorizo and where to drink cider poured from a great height. Near Almeria he turns off the main road and shows her where they used to make movies, Western movies. He was an extra once. "Maybe you saw me," he says. "I was an Indian, painted face and feathers in my hair. My hair was very long then.

"There were forty of us," he says, "riding and whooping. Some of us were supposed to fall off, but I couldn't do it. Held on right to the end."

"Look at this," Jaime says, walking through cities, villages, traveling down the coast road with the Mediterranean dancing blue far below.

"Look at this," Jaime says. "Remember this."

But mostly she notices his profile, driving in the car. Or the way sunlight falls on his left hand, resting on a wooden table under a leafy tree.

Sometimes at night they drive through distant towns, looking for a hotel. In the discreet ritual of a Catholic country, she waits in the car while Jaime arranges a room. No one wants to see her, although her passport must be examined, recorded. Sometimes in the car she thinks that her passport has checked in to hotels all over the country, that Jaime has traveled with her passport all over the country. Hair color, eyes, the essential data. A photograph that looks nothing at all like her.

Tengo hambre, tengo frío, tengo dolor.

The thing is that she is just passing through. On her way to somewhere. Friends are turning brown on the beaches of Greece; postcards arrive, pictures of fishermen mending yellow nets under a painful blue sky. She reads the cards in the echoing lobby of the main post office, jostled by brightly colored backpacks. A murmur of languages seeps around the edges of the lighted telephone *cabinas,* and she wonders what she is waiting for. Some days, postcard in hand, she begins the long walk to the station to ask about a ticket. But it is a very long walk; she stops for a cup of coffee along the way. Sees, without warning, the dark planes of Jaime's face as a match flares between his cupped hands.

She thinks then about staying. Manolo says she would have no trouble finding work; people are always looking for tutors, and there is an American school.

"I'll think about it," she says.

Jaime says nothing at all.

Sitting in the café across from the park, she asks herself what she is doing. Staying or not staying, looking for answers in the signs nailed to old trees. Reading between the lines of a grammar text. Pushing away the books, the pen, she takes a sip of cooling coffee and smooths out the newspaper. She tries to read it every day for practice. Tries to guess which stories would catch Jaime's eye, which headlines would make him pause, flipping through.

On this day it seems that something important has happened. Banner headlines and exclamations, a grainy photograph of a middle-aged man centered on the front page. She remembers that the photograph was visible, in different sizes, on all the newspapers clipped to the side of the kiosk. She assumes that he is dead but can't quite make it out. Peacefully in his sleep or in a blinding flash on a street corner; Franco has been dead for a year, and these things happen.

One particular word seems to be the key to the thing, appearing in different forms through all the related articles. *El secuestro, los se-cuestradores, secuestrar.* Nothing makes sense without this word. She flips through the vocabulary in the back of the textbook, but it isn't there. *I should know this,* she thinks, trying likely English words. Finding nothing.

"Javier," she says, calling him away from the mirror, "Javier, come here a minute. What's this word, what does this word mean?"

"Ah," Javier says, following her pointing finger. "*Secuestrar.* How to explain it? How do you say it—what do you call it, in English, when you catch someone and keep them, when you won't let them go until you have been given what you ask for?"

She tries to tell him, but suddenly she can't stop laughing.

ON THE BORDER

It was a hot day. He was killing chickens for all the old women, and the knife was sticky and terrible. He threw each severed bird to the ground, where it jerked and beat its wings, and when it was still a woman lifted it by one taut foot, holding it well away from her body. Dark splatters held down the dust in places. The other women stood together, shaded by the brims of their floppy hats, talking about children and grandchildren. And noticed suddenly that he lay facedown in the dust and the blood and the feathers, not moving. For a terrible moment it seemed that he had cut his own throat by mistake.

And then everything else was moving, everyone running; they turned him over and a foreign girl tried to make him breathe. She plucked a curled white feather from his chin before she covered his mouth with her own. The women's voices twittered above her head, and their splattered shadows bobbed and swooped at the edge of her vision. The tip of a long blond braid brushed his eyes. She saw that her hand had left a dusty streak across his face and she wanted to stop and wipe it off, but the nurse came and the ambulance, and they drove away in a great hurry although they knew there was no point. He was an old man, not given to troubling anyone; he died without a sound.

When they told his wife, two women stood to catch her as she fainted, as they had expected she would. They were in the laundry room; they eased her onto a pile of waiting sheets and dabbed her face with water from a sprinkler bottle. A large-bladed fan circled slowly over their heads. They straightened her thick glasses and led her to her room, one on either side and several behind. It was very quiet. They passed a man and a young boy digging in a garden, spades whispering through the dry earth.

It was a hot day, but the room was dark and cool. When they opened the front door the first things they saw were his slippers, side by side, waiting to be stepped into, and they thought Leah might faint again, but she didn't. They stayed with her through the long afternoon, speaking of all their losses, husbands and sons. Her neighbor, coming home, slipped through the net of hidden voices, feeling the handle of the door suddenly cool and smooth in his hand. His wife brushed out her long blond hair, and they lay down to sleep.

Later the widow began to wail and cry out loud. Next door the girl woke and turned to her husband; he lay on his back, lips slightly parted, and she closed her eyes against his sleeping mouth. On the other side of the wall someone told Leah to take a pill, and there was quiet.

The daughters arrived with the last bus from Jerusalem, late in the night. They spoke softly, made coffee and tea. One dropped a spoon and giggled like a child at the sudden sound. They walked about in their hard-soled shoes for hours, and their footsteps echoed, as in an empty house.

All the next day the widows came and went, carrying plates of biscuits and cakes, different soups. They walked her in front of the house, one cupping an elbow on either side. She was smaller than any of them.

In the late afternoon they carried Yoav down the winding road to the cemetery near the river. Some of the men had just come from the fields and red dust coated their shoes, legs. Leah moved like a sleepwalker between her two tall daughters. Her eyes behind the thick lenses were very pale, and her feet barely marked the ground. The place was ringed with eucalyptus trees grown tall, and long wild grasses, bamboo. To the east, the dusty hills of a hostile country. His friends made short speeches as the shadows crept in. They put Leah in a car with her daughters, and it was finished.

It was hot. August, the killing time. The floors of the rooms were tiled, smooth, and all the shutters were kept closed. Primitive air conditioners hummed, and the rooms were dim and almost cool. So hard to open a door and step outside in August. To step into light so bright; even the flowers, violent reds and yellows, attacked the eyes. To open a door and step outside, feel the heat wrapping around the body, sweat forming in the places between fingers, in every tiny crease. Every day the sun stabbed down from a hard blue sky. It had been so for months, every day as bad as the day before. Late in the afternoons a teasing breeze rattled the branches of palm trees, a warm breeze that died almost as it began. And always the night fell down, thick and still; nothing moved. People fought with their friends and punished their children, fell from ladders and tangled their hands in machinery. People stretched tighter and tighter, in August.

Leah came back from visiting with her daughters and said that someone had been in her room. She stood in her neighbors' kitchen kneading her fingers, one by one.

"You didn't hear anything?" she said. "You didn't see anything? Ask Allon when he comes home, maybe he knows."

"It's very odd," Allon's wife said later. "The key was with her, someone must have an extra key. The lock wasn't forced, I looked."

"Did they take anything?" Allon said, unbuttoning his shirt, running his hands through his dusty hair.

"That's also strange," she said, "they took strange things. An umbrella. Some old records. A wooden spoon. And she said that Yoav's clothes were all messed up, but she didn't think anything was missing."

"Tell her to speak to Ezra," Allon said. "Tell her to get him to change the lock."

"I already did," his wife said.

"Then that should be the end of it."

Later, when the long shadows stretched across the grass, Allon walked with Leah through the garden at the side of her room.

"Yoav took care of the garden," she said. "I don't know anything about it."

So Allon walked with her through the garden and named each

plant. He told her when to water, and exactly how much, although she didn't seem to be listening.

"It's a nice garden," he said. "Yoav made it very nice."

But she didn't seem to be listening.

The carpenter came home late and angry, slamming doors.

"Wasting my time," he said. "I can't take a step without some old woman wanting something."

He drank from a bottle of cold water and rammed it back into the refrigerator. It rattled icily beneath his words.

"Nothing wrong with the lock," he said. "I've got better things to do. Why would anyone want anything from her anyway?"

His wife studied psychology from educational television. She said, "It's natural, she's just lost Yoav, her security. It's symbolic, you see, having the locks changed."

The carpenter snorted and went to have a cold shower. The water was tepid and he cursed in several languages. His wife looked through the kitchen window and saw herself walking away with a white flower in her hair and a suitcase in her hand.

The night fell down, heavy and still. Allon's mother, moving through it, passed a lighted window. A young girl crossed a room, holding her heavy hair on top of her head with both hands. Her steps were violent, three strides across the room. Allon's mother walked faster; she was late for a meeting. But a caged girl paced through her mind.

The meeting room was thick with cigarette smoke and everyone was tired, and tired of trying to solve everyone else's problems. Typewritten requests stuck to their hands.

"We should talk about what to do with Leah," Allon's mother said.

"It's very sad," the younger women said. "It's always very sad. But she'll get over it, with time."

Their heads ached and their children were all crying somewhere and their husbands would all be in bed asleep when they got home. Allon's mother said, "I've known her more than thirty years, and she's never been able to get over anything, not without help. I remember when she came here. . . ."

The younger women sighed and lit more cigarettes. They knew the story, as they knew all the strange sad stories of the past. Grandparents disappearing beyond the range of the high arc lights, orders shouted in a harsh language. Parents jumping from moving trains, hiding in cellars, fighting over moldy crusts of bread. Leah appearing from the dark hole of Europe, a strange little thing, skittering along the dusty track like a frightened deer. She was somehow not all right, and they wanted to send her away. But Yoav, who never asked for anything, begged them to let her stay, swore that all he wanted in this life was to take care of her. The younger women knew the story, as they knew all those stories of the beginning. Sharing clothes and singing all night, fighting malaria and hacking in the dusty earth for hours. Years. They had heard it all before and they were tired; their heads ached and their eyes scratched and their children were all crying somewhere.

"Why don't we arrange for some course," the carpenter's wife said. "Something creative, something—"

"Let's discuss it next time," someone said. "It's very late."

"Next time," Allon's mother said.

Walking home, she thought of her second husband. Killed by a sniper's bullet down by the border. The day they were married the sky filled with strangely shaped clouds and they tried to read their future. They bought a sack of peanuts to share with the others, and began to eat them, walking down the winding road from town. Strange, but after thirty years the sound of her footsteps is the splintering of those shells. She can feel a dusty powder on her fingertips, almost taste them on her tongue.

Leah washed the front step over and over. She thought she saw footprints creeping to her front door, and no matter how many times she scrubbed and washed, they were there to lead her in.

Allon's blond wife peeled onions in the main kitchen. She sat on a low wooden chair; all around her giant steam pots hissed, and women shouted and banged heavy metal dishes. She recited a poem in her own language, something from school, a long time before. A pine bough caressed by falling snowflakes. Tears slipped from her eyes. "The onions," she said. Later she fainted and the women stroked her hot face and sent her home. Onion tears pressed at her eyes the whole way and she almost ran when she saw the front door. She splashed her face with cold water, holding it with her cupped hands. *Kjerstin,* she said. *My name is Kjerstin, and I come from a place where it snows in winter and you can read your words in the clear air.*

"Kjerstin," a voice said, "Kjerstin, are you there?"

It took her some moments to realize that the voice came from outside, that Leah was scrabbling at the door, wanting in.

"Look," Leah said, standing in the open doorway, reaching into the pocket of her faded dress. "Look, he's still getting in."

She held out a silver pen in a hard plastic case. Fiery needles danced straight to Kjerstin's eyes.

"It's not the same pen," Leah said. "Yoav gave it to me for a present. My name was engraved on it. Someone took it and put another in its place.

"What kind of person would do that," Leah said, turning away, letting the door close slowly.

"I think there's something wrong," Kjerstin said. "I think there's something very wrong."

She set a tray on a low table and sat down, her knee touching her husband's. "No one would do that, why would anyone do that? And last week she said that one of Yoav's undershirts was missing. She's not all right."

"Of course she's not," Allon said. "Her husband's suddenly dead and she's all alone.

"What would you do," Allon said, dropping a match into an ashtray just before it burned his fingers. "What would you do if I went off to the army and didn't come back?"

"I wouldn't spend all day counting your undershirts," she said, and he smiled and spooned too much sugar into his coffee cup.

Allon drove through the fields all day in a rattling jeep. Checking irrigation lines, opening and closing valves, soaked by the foul-smelling river water and steaming dry in the August sun, over and over again. Almost every day he drove past the place where a bullet found his father, and he wondered why on this day he had stopped to think of it.

The border patrol found footprints near the fence as the sun was going down. The men picked up their guns and went off to guard the perimeter, the children's houses; it happened from time to time. The static from their radios carried a long way, and orange flares lit the sky.

The carpenter's wife packed a small suitcase and hid it under the bed. She went out into the crackling night to look at her youngest son, who dreamed terrible things. Looking down at his sleeping face, she thought that she might weaken after all, and take him with her.

Allon's mother was translating an article for the newspaper. She spoke five languages easily; before Independence she had walked through dangerous countries in various disguises, setting up escape routes. As a girl of fifteen she had moved through an occupied city, carrying guns in her hollowed-out schoolbooks. Now she lifted her hands from the typewriter and rubbed at her tired eyes, knowing that the shutters were closed. She heard the colored flares rising and remembered a night in '48. Remembered sitting alone in a dark room, listening to the pounding of the long guns and letting herself think for a moment that they could never survive.

Something scratched at Kjerstin's door very late.

"Don't be afraid, it's Leah, it's only me."

She was wrapped in a cotton robe, her hair tumbled, her eyes small and vulnerable without her glasses. Kjerstin couldn't bear to look at her: the same cringing feeling that came when she saw Leah's faded underwear hanging on a line by the front door.

"Everything's dark," Leah said. "I plugged in the kettle and everything went out, what should I do?"

"It's probably just a fuse," Kjerstin said, slipping an old letter between the pages of a book. "Do you have extra fuses?"

"What do they look like," Leah said. "I don't know, Yoav fixed everything, I don't know what to do. Can you go to find some-one?"

"Let me try," Kjerstin said.

Next door in Leah's room it was already stuffy and very hot. A tall candle burned in the kitchen, the only light. Kjerstin climbed on a chair and began trying fuses. Leah's wild-haired shadow danced on the wall. With the sound of each flare rising, she jumped and twitched.

"I hate the noise," she said, "I hate that noise. Like the war, like all the wars, with the big guns at night. Yoav is gone and no one can help me now, he'll find me now."

The fuse connected and the room jumped out at them, but Leah didn't seem to notice. She was staring down at her hands, rubbing her palms together hard.

"It was an accident," she said. "We didn't intend . . . he was a lit-tle man with broken teeth. He must have been lost. It was in the war, he was all alone, driving down the road. We ambushed his truck. We only wanted the petrol, we didn't know what to do with him. We had no place for prisoners, no food for prisoners. He sat on the floor with his hands tied behind his back, crying and shak-ing, and I said I would shoot him."

The only sound was the rubbing of her wrinkled hands.

"It's all right," Kjerstin said softly. "I've fixed it, Leah, and the noise has stopped, and it's not dark anymore."

"Why can't he leave me alone," Leah said as she closed the door. As the lock clicked.

When she first came to this place, Kjerstin saw everything. A man wheeling a baby carriage with a machine gun balanced on top. Concrete bunkers grown over with flowers and children's paintings. Now, when Allon put on his green uniform and disappeared for a few days, a few weeks, she thought only that she would miss him while he was gone. Nights like this, when the sky was bright and the patrols were out, when anything could happen, she picked up a book and waited to hear that it was over.

It was a hot day, and the carpenter came into the dining room angry. He sat down at a table with some friends and said, "That's it. It's too much. It's craziness, that's all it is."

His friends said, "What do you care? Put in a few locks and keep the old woman quiet, what's the problem?"

An old man stood up, pushed in his chair. He was remembering a stormy meeting near the beginning. Fists crashing on the table, making the coffee cups chatter. Yoav standing up and saying, in his quiet way, that the day there was a lock anywhere on the kibbutz would be the day he left.

"Things change," the old man said, but no one heard.

The carpenter finished his dinner, smoked a cigarette, and felt better. He crossed the cool dining room to tell Leah that he would put small hooks inside all the windows. But he wouldn't change the lock again. It was new, and expensive, and he had other things to do.

Allon's wife wrapped her blond braids about her head, and they walked through bright flowers to his mother's room. It was Friday and the place was noisy with children and grandchildren, eating and drinking.

"When did Leah tell you this?" Allon's mother said.

"The night they shot the terrorists."

"Ah," Allon's mother said, as if everything was explained.

"Is it true?"

"I don't know," Allon's mother said. "We had prisoners here once or twice in forty-eight, some Iraquis, I remember. By accident, really. We never killed them, we sent them on as soon as we could, that's all. But Leah spent some time in another place, it may have happened there. I doubt it, but who knows. We were all on one border or another all those years. Things happen in a war."

"But she is really frightened," Kjerstin said. "She thinks the prisoner has come back for her, she thinks now that Yoav's gone, he's come back for her."

"Nonsense," Allon's mother said. "She's always been afraid of something. Afraid that her children would hurt themselves playing games. Afraid that there wasn't enough flour and we would all be hungry again. I've discussed it with the health committee; there's really nothing we can do. And she's still working, she still comes to the dining room. Actually, she's managing better than I thought she would."

"But she's not," Kjerstin said.

"Ezra's wife thinks she should take up macramé and find herself," Allon's mother said.

"Ezra's wife watches too much television," someone said, and they laughed.

Allon's mother served coffee in glass cups and opened the windows.

"We're all being spoiled," she said. "There's nothing so terrible about a little night air, nothing wrong with being a little uncomfortable. We lived for years without even dreaming of air-conditioning. We survived."

The August heat oozed into the room. Allon lay on the floor with his two small nephews. They rolled a sponge ball back and forth; tiny bells were sewn inside, a clear, clean sound.

On a hot day Leah climbed three stone steps to ask the security officer for a gun. A small pistol, something. The security officer was washing his hands outside the dining room. He had been up most of the night. His wife was sleeping with his neighbor, and his oldest son wore a diamond earring, and all he wanted was to be sitting down in a cool room somewhere. He raised his voice and shook water from his hands, and Leah ran like a frightened deer.

When the carpenter's wife heard the story that evening, she nodded and began to talk about phallic symbolism, but she heard her own voice, and stopped.

"Someone should call her daughters," she said. "Maybe she needs to get away for a while, maybe she just needs a change."

"Tell it to the health committee," Ezra said. "I'm tired."

His wife turned out the light and thought that the summer would never end.

September was a slow, drawn-out sigh. A few white clouds appeared, small but promising. People sat out in the evenings, sipping iced drinks, quiet voices like the rustling of leaves on the trees. The carpenter's wife unpacked her suitcase and Allon's mother began to knit a small white blanket. Leah's old underwear danced on the line, making Allon's wife laugh out loud, although she was by herself. People began to recognize one another and waited for the rain, and the afternoon breeze smoothed the lines from their faces.

The prisoner came sometime during a cool night. In the morning one of the widows called, "Leah, wake up, it's late." Knocking on the front door. Later she said, "I knew before I even looked inside; it was the sound of an empty house."

It was six o'clock and the grass was still damp; her sandals left faint marks on the tiled floor. The room was murky, only the light that slipped through the open window.

Leah sat in a chair in a pale circle of light by the window. Into the silence came the sound of her quiet breathing. Her glasses lay on the floor beside the chair, and her empty eyes were terrible. They took her away in an ambulance, and no one was particularly surprised.

MAX—1970

///

M ax's father is teaching him how to fix the dishwasher. It is not going well. Saturday afternoon, a dead gray sky through the kitchen window, through the bare branches of the lilac tree. Something like opera on the radio. Max thinks that any minute now he will have to scream.

It's not like there's anything really wrong with the dishwasher. A low hum at the end of the rinse cycle, a few streaks on the plates and glasses. Surely not enough to merit this savagery, the way it has been disemboweled on the off-white linoleum, wires hanging loose. An open toolbox full of things that have names Max can't even guess at.

In the living room his mother is fitting his sisters' costumes and he can hear them twittering, the occasional squeal when a pin scrapes the skin. He pictures their pigtails flicking against their shoulders. It's Halloween and they're going out as angels—what a joke. Max is tapping his foot on the floor, the frayed bell of his jeans almost covering his running shoe. Three inches away from his father's nose, where he's peering at something under the machine, and Max knows the tapping will be driving him crazy but he can't stop. He sees the way his father's hair is growing back in strange, tufty patches, nothing like it used to be, and he looks out the window instead. Then up to the clock above it. He was on his way out to the plaza when his father appeared with the toolbox. Typical, the way they're always going on at him about making new friends and then telling him there's some stupid job to be done. With his father home from the hospital he doesn't have to look after his sisters so much, but they just don't understand how things work here.

"Why don't you invite them over to listen to some records," his mother says in that new cheerful voice she has.

By now they'll all be gathered behind Woolworth's, rolling cigarettes and striking matches on the beige brick. No one will notice that he's not there, and even if they did, they wouldn't wonder about it. They'll move on somewhere without him, and at the moment this seems incredibly tragic.

"Well, look at this," his father says, and Max squats down, peering at a mess of wires and trying to see what's caused all the excitement.

"Do you see," his father says, and Max says, "Yeah, sure."

As he stands up, there's a sudden jerk and a pain in his scalp that brings tears to his eyes, a chunk of his long hair snagged around a nut or a screw or whatever the damn thing is.

"Oh shit," he says before he can stop himself, but his father doesn't seem to notice, says, "What happened? Max—hold still, don't panic. I'll get the scissors."

"No scissors!" Max shrieks, and as he does there's a sudden memory of a chair in the middle of the kitchen in their old house, the teakettles on the yellowed wallpaper, his feet swinging off the floor, the buzz of his father's electric clippers.

"Hold still," his father says, as if he had a choice, and now all Max can see is his father's fingers, gently unwinding. He can't remember ever looking at his father's hands but he's sure they weren't like this. So pale they're almost greenish, shaking a little. Punctures and bruises on the back from his last hospital stay, and Max thinks suddenly that it must hurt. Then he is free, rubbing at his scalp, a few blond strands wrapped tightly around an evil-looking bolt.

"If you'd get a haircut, that wouldn't happen," his father says, and Max thumps his feet as he leaves the room. He meets his mother in the hallway and she stops him by putting one hand on his shoulder, he can feel the anger leaving him, as if she's drawing it out with that hand.

"There are just things you have to know, Max," his father says when he comes back to the kitchen.

"I already know how to use the Yellow Pages," Max says, but then he throws up his hands and says, "Just kidding," and his father lets it go.

Neither one of them has the patience for this, and Max wonders why he's the only one who seems to know it.

While Max puts the tools away, his father hooks the dishwasher hose onto the tap. He can hear his sisters bouncing a ball against the wall of the house as his father turns the dial. The low hum is gone, but in its place there's a loud metallic rattle. Max looks up sideways from his crouch and sees his father's still back, his right hand reaching slowly to turn the dial again, turn off the tap. He walks from the room, and Max hears the back door close quietly. With a sigh he wheels the dishwasher to the middle of the floor and unscrews the back again, then realizes he has no idea what to do next. Looking through the back door, he sees his father sitting on the cold lawn, one hand pulling up little chunks of grass and letting them fall slowly from his grasp. After what seems like a long time Max's sisters appear, running. They throw themselves on their father, wrapping their arms around his neck. Then they all stand up and Max moves away before they turn around.

In the shower he tries a couple of numbers, using the soap as a microphone, but his heart doesn't seem to be in it. He plops the white washcloth on top of his head and folds his lips over his teeth, checking in the hazy shower mirror; his eyes startle him. Then he notices something red and bulging right in the middle of his chin, and he peers more closely.

"Oh shit," he says and hears his sisters gasp outside, the sound of running feet. "Spies," he shouts, opening the door and releasing a swirl of steam. "I'm surrounded by spies!"

It's late when Max arrives at the party and he wanders from room to room, the music pulsing through him. He's covered his face with white makeup, almost sure that the spot on his chin is invisible. Hair slicked back, lipstick blood dripping around his mouth.

"You look sweet," a girl named Judy says, dancing by.

"I'm *Dracula,* for Chrissake," he says, but she's already gone.

He keeps walking around until he finds the back door and lets himself out, keeps moving. He walks around the Crescents and the Roads and the Drives, under the cold stars. He misses his friend Rob and the way they used to race their bikes, the way they knew every tree, every blade of grass in town. All the things they never had to say to each other. The letters they write once in a while aren't the same, aren't even worth doing, really.

Once, when they were in fourth grade, their teacher pulled the world map down over the blackboard and then showed them a book with maps the explorers had drawn hundreds of years ago. After they'd all laughed at the sizes and shapes, she told them to think about how hard it would be to make a map if you didn't already know how the world looked, or if you couldn't look down from a great distance. In the weeks before the moving truck came, Max walked around his town with a mapmaker's eye, memorizing every mound, every secret path. The distance from his doorway to his bed, the exact pattern of the cracks on the ceiling.

Max walks around the side of their little house to the backyard and sits down at the picnic table he should have put away weeks ago. Smokes a cigarette and wonders if his mother will comment on the smell of his clothes. There's no way of knowing what she'll choose to get worked up about these days. She was as bad as his sisters during supper, thinking she heard someone at the door, stepping over the toolbox as she got up to peek around the corner, and coming back, laughing at herself. Fussing about whether she'd bought enough candy.

"Next year I'll have a better idea," she said, "it's just all so different here, I don't know what to expect."

Something in her voice that Max had never heard before when she was talking to him, something in the tone and the way she met his eyes, like they were on a level.

All around him there are sounds of the neighborhood shutting down. A garage door closing, the rattle of a garbage-can lid. A low whistle and the chinking of a dog's collar. There are things he can't help thinking about. The sound of his mother's shoes falling by the front door when she pulls them off after work. The way his sisters with their floating hair really did look like angels. The way his father used to play catch with him long after supper, the way the ball loomed out of the dark in the split second before it smacked into his glove, and how even if they could do that again, it wouldn't be the same. He wants suddenly, desperately, to be any age but what he is, to be anyone else.

His fingers are numb, and he flicks his butt over the low hedge for the people with the Siamese cats to find. His own house is dark except for the neon haze that comes from the top of the stove, the orange light over the back door, glowing to guide him in. He tries to imagine that this moment is long in the past, tries to imagine where he will be, what he will be doing, on a Saturday night in October in ten years, in twenty or thirty.

Of all the things he might have considered, he never could have guessed that it would be this. Feeling the thick, humid air of a foreign country as it oozes through an open window, bringing with it the sound of calling voices, of traffic that never stops. Standing on a shaky ladder while a long-haired woman steadies the base. Holding three colored wires that dangle from a hole in the ceiling, trying frantically to remember something his father once said. Certain that if he gets it wrong, the whole world will go up in a blaze of light.

BY THE SEA,
BY THE SEA

*Each physician should counsel those over whom he has advisory charge
of the dangers incident to a prolonged exposure in the ocean.*

—British Medical Journal, *1904.*

*. . . and on Tuesday I called on the poor McIntyres, whose daughter
Mary died of overbathing last summer in Ostend.*

—W. Lumsden, Rambles Through the Shires, *1906.*

You have probably seen photographs of Mary McIntyre, you
may even have one on the wall in your den, or in a box under
the stairs. Sometimes she stands at the back, one hand resting on
someone's shoulder, or sometimes she sits beside others on a set-
tee, staring straight ahead. She's the one you can't imagine smiling,
although in fact she had a lovely smile.

Her clothes are unremarkable. You can't see the colors, but they are usually shades of brown and beige. Her mother has always preferred brown, and she chooses the fabric; it has never really occurred to her that the tones she loves may not be the best for Mary, whose hair is the color of tea with not enough milk. It looks darker in the photographs. Drawn back smoothly, making her face look even rounder, and her eyes appear dark too, although they were really a flat bluish-gray.

Unless you looked very closely you probably would not notice that her left shoulder is a little higher than the right, the result of a slightly twisted spine, perhaps an accident of birth. Half an inch higher, say, which does not sound like much, does not even look like much when you bring out the old wooden ruler from your desk drawer. But it was a lot for Mary McIntyre; it may explain everything about Mary McIntyre. Or it may explain nothing at all, it may be incidental and have nothing to do with the things that happened. But someone should understand, or try to. Someone should know about Mary McIntyre and how she looked in that long dress. Someone should know about that summer in Ostend and the way she vanished from the pictures.

The Channel crossing was rough and her mother's head ached and there was trouble with the luggage when they landed and her father had to make a scene, even though he hated to, because it was so often the only way. Afterward he went out walking to calm himself and her mother rested and Mary McIntyre sat in a chair by her open window, listening to the soft *shush* of the sea and trying to make out its oily black surface by the light of the stars. Perhaps she thought about a new place, a new start, or perhaps that never occurred to her. She was a dreamer, something you wouldn't have guessed from looking at her, and often in her dreams she sat just so in a sunny garden, or walked a sandy path, carrying her bonnet by the strings in one hand. In the house where she grew up every sneeze made her mother flinch, every bump or scrape would have Mary in bed with blankets and potions, a cool hand on her forehead testing for fever. Perhaps she learned it early, this retreat into dreams. Or perhaps it was always her way.

Things might have been different if the others had lived. Childbirth was never easy for her mother; her father heard the screams, pacing downstairs or out in the street, and wondered what kind of brute would come to a woman again after that. He tried, he did try, but the tiny stones were planted in the churchyard one by one until Mary lived a year and then two and they began to believe she was real. Not quite whole, perhaps, although they never would have said that, even to each other. The slight curve in her spine that caused pain from time to time; and the way she was—not simple, not that, but somehow removed. She could read and write and figure, she could learn anything if she put her mind to it, but she didn't often try, and to keep her attention fixed on a piece of sewing, a little polite conversation, was next to impossible. At times she said the most peculiar things. A stranger would notice it, a number did that summer in Belgium, but her parents gave no sign.

So here they are at breakfast the next morning, Mother a little pale but otherwise recovered and Father rubbing his hands together before picking up his fork and Mary McIntyre saying that she will not, after all, go into the sea that day.

She doesn't know why she has said it. Her father raises his eyebrows and says, "Very well," and she knows that he will talk about the weather a little and perhaps remark that the dining room is not so crowded at this hour. Then he will mention the cloudless sky again, and say that they have come here so that she can bathe and take the sea air, and then he will pause so she can explain why she won't go into the sea, but she won't be able to. Perhaps it is a premonition. Or perhaps a dream she had once, and in that dream she reached out a hand underwater and someone turned to her very slowly; she saw the face and woke screaming. Although no one came running, so perhaps the screaming was only inside the dream.

She knows that they have come here for her, rather than to Margate or Lowestoft like other years, and she knows that it is only partly for the sea air. More to avoid those familiar faces who ask after her aunt and uncle, who cluck their tongues over her cousin Charlie and inquire after her own health, having heard something of her collapse. Perhaps her parents are also tired of being reminded but she does not really think of that, so bound is she by her strange, dreamy pain, so used to the way they take care of her. So certain that this rift in the family is all her fault.

Everyone thought it was the first time. The shrieks and loud voices in the attic, the closed door of her room. They didn't know—did they know that it had been going on for years? Charlie saying, "Can we go and play?" Her mother's face smiling at where they stood, her aunt too, saying, "Run along now, off you go." The way she longed to step back into their safe world, to take one step over the drawing room threshold, and the way she knew it was impossible to do that. Their distant smiling faces in the steam from the silver pot and Charlie tugging at her hand, drawing her off to the garden, the shed, the attic.

"This is what people do," Charlie said, although he had only the haziest of notions. Pictures in those books hidden behind the shelves in his father's study. Mary McIntyre's poor pale flesh was nothing like the women in the books, but she kept still like he told her to, and after a time he discovered that it was better if he hurt her a little. How did her mother not notice, rubbing different oils over her crooked back? Even in the flickering light she must have seen the bruises on Mary's arms and thighs, in the hollows of her collarbone. Charlie saw them himself sometimes, and felt a little ashamed and more than a little amazed at his power. Once he gave her some sweets, flecked with lint from his pocket.

When they were discovered Mrs. McIntyre felt her hands go cold, and she looked at her brother, his face transformed by rage and his eyes flicking to hers and immediately away again. She'd never told a soul about those times he'd held her down when they were young, the pain and his sweaty boy-smell. In that flick of the eyes it all came back and she almost screamed at his whiskered face, the cake crumbs on his vest, the white napkin still clutched in one hand. Just for a moment and then Mrs. McIntyre heard herself speaking calmly, but no one else seemed to, the bluster and the noise and Mary weeping, Charlie cuffed out of the house and down the street, her sister-in-law gasping into her handkerchief.

Things might have been different then. Marooned in her room, Mary McIntyre slept and slept yet still somehow felt she was waking. Until Charlie was sent to a new school where he caught diphtheria and quickly died; then some horror knocked her from her feet and rolled her about without mercy. Months passed that are lost to her now, although their story may be hidden in the lines around her mother's mouth, the dark smudges that will remain beneath her eyes for the rest of her life.

———

Someone should know about Mary McIntyre and how she felt that first morning at Ostend, for she did go to bathe in the sea; there was never really any question. Her parents waited on the shore, sitting straight in their rented chairs, and someone should have heard Mary's teeth chatter as she pulled on her costume, known the smell of wet wood and dried salt and the shock that went through her at the first touch of the sea's cold hand, the cold licking tongues of the sea welcoming her back.

She'd been to the seaside before, of course, and paddled for hours when she and Charlie were children. Every year their families had holidayed in Folkestone, in Lowestoft or Margate. By the time she was old enough to look forward to things, they were getting ready to change, but there were still a few years when Charlie looked after her well, tipping a bucket to make a sand tower, helping her stand when she had fallen, although he was only half a head taller himself.

In those days it was always hot and clear, and she remembers people sitting around a table and her father's mustache moving as he says that you couldn't get better weather anywhere, not even in the tropics. The men swam every morning and the children splashed at the water's edge and even her mother once took off her stockings and clenched her toes in the sand. The end of an afternoon, holding Charlie's sticky hand, grains of sand rubbing between their fingers. The sun still warm on the top of her head, for she carries her bonnet by its strings, and no one tells her that she must put it on. Her father and uncle walk in front, their shirtsleeves rolled up, and her mother and aunt come behind, holding on to each other and laughing at something, perhaps the way their feet keep slipping. In a moment she and Charlie will say that their legs are tired, and their fathers will bend down from their great height and swing them up through the air. But it is the moment just before this that she recognizes in some way. The hot sun, the waves, the faint sound of a band playing somewhere, and the tall, gentle shapes surrounding; it is this moment that hovers at the edge of all her dreams.

So it cannot be the novelty of the sea that explains what happened that summer, and not the seaside either. A foreign one, it's true, but one large hotel is much like another, and the promenade, the pier. Differences perhaps in the sanitary arrangements, but even these are not so great. And the sound of French, of German and even Flemish, but as her mother remarked last time at Margate, with the babble of accents one might as well have been in a foreign country.

What was it, then, that made everything seem strange and strangely charged? Perhaps she was changing, Mary McIntyre, that is, perhaps she was on the verge of some great stepping out. Perhaps if death had not stepped in she would have clasped her life and run with it. Or perhaps it was oily death all the time, sidling closer, nudging her shoulders, her chest, twining around. Perhaps that was the thing that colored it all.

Someone should know about Mary McIntyre, yet it's so hard to keep her in focus. Her outline blurs, as it does in those photographs, as she herself faded out. The sound of her voice no more than a murmur against the tinkling of silver spoons on saucers, the competing bands from the park, the pier, from the great hall of the Kursaal. It becomes harder and harder to know her first thoughts as she comes awake in the mornings, to know her mind in the dining room as she cuts carefully at her meat while the fair-haired waiters move soundlessly from table to table. The midday sun darts now and then through the high windows, sparking on cutlery already polished to gleaming, and it strikes the lines around her father's eyes, the cords in the thinning neck above his collar, and she sees that he is growing old, that perhaps he will die soon and that even then things will not really change. She will trail behind her mother forever, from place to place, in and out of season, and the thought makes her incredibly weary, leaves her without the strength to lift her fork to her mouth.

Across the table her father works his tongue at a bit of gristle lodged in his back teeth; as far as he is concerned, foreign meat is always suspect, although he keeps this conviction to himself. He is a decent, baffled man who fears he has misstepped somewhere. He thinks of bells and white clouds and his wife's hand on his arm and remembers that he felt ready to take on the world. Now the sunlight through the windows is uncomfortably warm; he watches his daughter daydreaming, her fork halfway to her lips, and wonders how he could have forgotten to do that.

Mrs. McIntyre is also uneasy about the meat but supposes she will get used to it. She is a woman of hidden but strong opinions who should have had more to organize than a small household, rounds of visiting, occasional excursions in season. Who might have, in fact, if all those gravestones hadn't battered the life out of her, left her watching her living child dreaming again, with a helpless mixture of love and despair. Mary's hair pulled back smoothly, covering her ears, which fold out a little at the top just like her father's, her face inclined to plumpness without the bloom of health, and her awkward mouth, again so like her father's that her mother can't help thinking of all those small bodies, how one or two had thatches of her own dark hair, how things might have been different.

She stops those thoughts though, just as she stops the pang she feels at the sight of her own mottled hand reaching out to take a roll from the basket. The rolls are fresh and slightly warm; everything here is as it should be, and the waiters anticipate every need without intruding. This is the only way she knows to keep chaos at bay. Breakfast and a stroll, luncheon and a rest, perhaps a concert in the evening. Life can proceed in a strange hotel much as it does at home. She knows that only marriage will be the saving of her daughter, and the sight of her own aging hand suggests that it is not too soon to think about that, to make the acquaintance of some of those mothers whose sons trail, reluctantly or attentively, through the reading room, the picture gallery.

Looking at her husband, his cheek bulging as he works at his teeth, she counts her blessings. She would have done anything to get away from the home where she lived under the shadow of her brothers, and sometimes under their weight. It was just luck, really, that her husband was still as he had seemed when she first met him—a kind, serious man who took care of things but rarely interfered. He would agree, she is sure, that it is time to think about Mary's future, about committing her to someone else's care. Perhaps, in one way of thinking, a European would be quite suitable. Less likely to remark the long silences, the occasional blurting out of strange things. And that business with Charlie—but she stops that thought as quickly as it flashes across her mind. She does, however, permit herself a brief dream of some years hence. A courtly son-in-law and the soft curls of grandchildren, the way they smell when she hugs them close.

As it turned out none of that happened and Mrs. McIntyre herself was dead within the year, so the dreary round of days that Mary foresaw would not come to be either. Although it may have, if she herself hadn't stepped from the picture. The final shape of the puzzle determined by each piece slotting in in a particular way, a particular order.

What happened next will be recorded in a stack of dusty records somewhere, a chance combination of streams and currents that comes once or twice a century to the coast around Ostend. The air remained cool, but the sea became warmer and warmer and seemed to deepen its color, the blues and greens as intense as jewels. The breeze on the shore carried the faintest hint of spice and a barely perceptible rattling, clacking sound. And while her parents sat up straight on the beach in their rented chairs, Mary McIntyre gave herself to the sea again and again. It rolled her around, it rolled around her, she paddled in the shallow warm water and even ducked right under, pulling herself clumsily at first with her arms, her struggling feet, but finally opening her eyes and seeing many things clearly.

Back on the shore where her parents wait it grows crowded and noisy, hawkers everywhere. Her father wishes he'd brought his pipe; he'd thought about it but assumed there would be too much wind, too much trouble fumbling with matches and tobacco. There is a wind, but a mild one, whispering over his cheek, barely ruffling the sleeve of his wife's dress. They have marked the position of their daughter's ocher-colored bathing machine, and a good thing too, for after an hour the sea is dotted with them and several are a similar shade. He pulls out his watch and remarks that the driver is over time again, not knowing that the driver is quite content to tarry if someone slips him a half franc along with the bathing coupon. Mrs. McIntyre says that she supposes that a few extra minutes won't matter, that the bathing seems to be doing a world of good, Mary's complexion is clearer and her back hasn't ached for days. Meeting her husband's eyes she smiles and he does too, until a newspaper vendor taps him on the shoulder, offering yet another copy of *La Chronique*.

Someone should know about Mary McIntyre and what she thought or sensed, looking out on that vast expanse of scented sea. Looking out toward Margate as she had looked out in other years from Margate, looking out on herself looking out and knowing that she was different. If she cupped her hands around her eyes and looked through, she could have been the last person in the world, or the only one, and if she had thought about it, she would have been surprised that this didn't frighten her. Quite the opposite, in fact.

When her extra time was up, she left her costume in a heap, her stockings sticking a little as she pulled them on because she hadn't taken the time to dry properly, so eager was she, in those first few days, to open the door and step out, to carry it all with her into the world.

The mothers had arranged for her to walk the Digue with a boy named Gaston in the afternoon, and so they strolled with other couples, with families and groups of girls and young men. Gaston stroked his spotty mustache and spoke of his delicate health, the many treatments taken, and he recited some verses he had written that he was quite proud of, but allowed that perhaps they suffered in English. It was very warm; perspiration beaded the sides of her nose, her upper lip, and Gaston ran a finger beneath his collar. Looking out at the rows of different-colored bathing machines, she remarked that they were just like people, really, and he wrinkled his pale brow.

As they walked on, she felt impatience building until she could have screamed with it. To have this unyielding surface beneath her feet. To be hearing about Gaston's frail constitution when she felt herself bursting with good health, with luck. She thought of those walks taken to the cemetery with her mother for as long as she could remember. The creak of the gate, the quiet prayers, the two tears that crept down her mother's cheeks. Sometimes it surprised her that there were only two, and sometimes that there were still two. But she had not joined those tiny mounds in the churchyard; she had survived and she felt that as a triumph now, instead of a monstrous error.

Someone should know about Mary McIntyre and the way she closed her eyes, breathing in, hearing the sighing water, the far-off voices, and the closer call of seabirds. Feeling the way her heart slowed down, her rough edges smoothed out.

That morning they had gone to the lace market in the Place d'Armes, her father slipping away immediately to the reading room in search of an English newspaper. Her mother met Gaston's and they made slow progress through the market, stopping frequently to exclaim and rub things between their fingers. Gaston remained stubbornly by Mary's side, carrying a few packages and fumbling for his white handkerchief. Out of sight of the water she was dazed, she hardly heard a word he said. Straining for the sound of the waves, for the call of those wheeling birds. She began to realize that it had become an urgent thing, that some balance had shifted so slyly she hadn't even noticed when it had happened. Harsh sunlight bounced back from the buildings lining the square, and loud voices and laughter beat at her ears. She tried to call on whatever the sea had given her, the ease in her manner that made her mother smile and pat her hand, the sense of becoming that made each new day a welcome thing. But it had gone, it was gone, and she was left a jagged shell in a hard-edged world, not knowing if she would scream or weep.

So she says some words to Gaston, she doesn't even know what words, and turns and walks quickly away from the square, from the town, walking faster and faster until she hears only the rasping slide of her soft shoes. Gaston starts after her, but she moves so fast, he hasn't really heard what she said, perhaps she is ill, he looks back to where he last saw his mother, searches for her lavender hat, looks back to see the flick of Mary McIntyre's brown skirt as she disappears around a far corner, and coughs briskly into his white handkerchief, wondering what to do.

At lunch Mary explained that she had suddenly felt ill, that the bathing had restored her and she was quite fine now, only a little tired. Later her mother placed her silver brush on the dressing table and said that she supposed it was all right, and her father said he thought Gaston a poor sort of fellow anyway. They agreed she was getting older, that perhaps they should let go a little, and they agreed the bathing seemed to make her happy, and that, after all, was what they had come for. After that Mary McIntyre went down to the beach twice a day and sometimes more, and the drivers began to watch out for her and her extra half franc. On the promenade her mother took her father's arm, and he bent his head in his courtly way to hear something she had said.

The sea stayed warm and it was warmer on the shore now and they all rested in the afternoons. Gaston and his mother returned to Liège, where he would soon meet the pale woman who would become his first wife. He will bury her and two others, clutching his white handkerchief in a changing world, and as an old man he will come back to Ostend to consult another specialist, will sit in a waiting room in a stray shaft of sunlight and wonder at his sudden unease, at the thought that things could have been different. Then someone will call his name and he will stop trying to remember whatever it is that he has forgotten.

And Mary McIntyre slept without resting, moaned and kicked in the underwater light of her room, the green shutters closed against the afternoon sun. Her appetite dwindled and a doctor, strolling past her on the terrace with his hands clasped behind his back, might have noticed, fleetingly, the light in her eyes, the color in her face. The air was warm and one day, hurrying to dress for dinner, she opened her wardrobe and caught a glimpse of blue between the brown and beige sleeves and pulled out a shimmering dress like nothing she had ever seen. The way it fell about her, the ripples of color like deep water splashed with sunlight; her hands trembled as she hooked it up.

In the dining room she thanked her mother and talked on and on, her eyes sparkling and her cheeks flushed. Raising the fork to her lips and putting it down untasted. And across the table Mrs. McIntyre felt a cold hand at her heart and knew that this was what she had been waiting for.

If someone had seen Mary McIntyre in that blue dress, things might still have been different. If someone had held out a human hand, even then, she might have known at once the truth about the soft fingers of the sea. But no one did. The dining room was full, people talked and laughed over the faint sound of the waves outside the dark windows. The fair-haired waiters stepped softly between the tables, their thoughts far away in their own countries. Like pieces in a jigsaw puzzle, each fit where it did, creating the perfect space for the one that came after, and the one after that. And some-time during the night the sly currents shifted, rolled back to slide onto white sand shores, beneath clattering palm trees.

By morning Mary was delirious with fever; they sent for Dr. Garnier, who shook his head, and then there was nothing left but the watching and waiting.

Someone should know about Mary McIntyre, but no one ever will. She remains as remote, as mysterious, as the person who sits next to you on the crowded bus, brushes past you on a busy street. Even someone who was right there could only guess at the things she dreams on the steps of her bathing machine, in her rumpled bed. The things she goes on dreaming. Dreaming the beach at Ostend, a cool wind brushing her cheeks, combing through her loosened hair. Dreaming the wild smell of the sea, the cries of spinning birds. Dreaming that her life will go on and on, that she will be there until the story ends.

AT THE RIVER

M y mother said, *Don't go down to the river,* said, *Don't go down to the river, don't go down to the river.*

Summer morning, screen door snap, smell of fresh-cut grass. My bike was a horse named Black Star, and I galloped through the town, left her grazing on the riverbank.

My mother said a girl she knew went down to the river and never came back again.

My mother said, *don't go down to the river,* but I didn't lie because I never said I wouldn't. I wore a long gray dress and a bonnet, and she would always remember the last time she saw me.

Down by the river there were pine trees growing with branches that swept the ground. Inside were caves for hiding or sitting. It was never lonely down by the river. Games were dangerous, never knowing the rules, always being picked last. Much better to wander alone, down by the river.

My mother had lines that drew her face down; she was always digging a fist into her back. Sometimes she blew soap bubbles high into the branches of trees, but not often.

The river was frozen, and on the other side the trees cased in ice were dazzling in the sun. I took a big stick to test the way and started across. Everything was silent in the snow.

My mother said children drowned in the river, all of them calling their mothers. Sometimes I thought I heard them, but it might have been just the wind.

I picked a bunch of yellow flowers that grew down by the water's edge. The river ran swift and deep there, the bottom a mass of waving green. When I fell, the flowers scattered on top.

My mother said, *Don't go down to the river,* and I thought she would know just by looking at me. When she didn't, I went back again and again, until I knew each tree, each stone in the path.

If you go left instead of right, you come to the dam near the bridge in the center of town. Big boys take off their shoes and socks and walk across with the water pushing at their ankles. I waited until I was all alone to try.

My brother swings in the garden. He's only little, and his laugh bubbles like the river flowing, like soap bubbles rising to the trees.

We have a horse named Bess and a horse named Paint; they pull the plow and the cart. I bring the cows in at night, and the heavy grass soaks my dress. Sometimes my brother helps; he's older than me, but simple. He likes to bang on the gate with an iron bar and call each cow by name.

—

My father came back from the war, but he left his leg behind. A stranger in the living room, giving me a bristly hug. His crutches lean on the wall by the supper table, but sometimes he stays in bed and my mother carries up a rattling tray. She calls him Tom and me her little darling.

One night we sat outside with blankets and watched men walk on the moon. My mother said I would tell my grandchildren about it, but I didn't grow up to be that old.

Through the fallow field with the long grass tickling and down a little hill, go right a ways along the riverbank, and you come to my special tree cave. Often in school I imagine myself sitting there, and I get in trouble for not paying attention. At school the big boys spill your water and you have to fill up the jar again from the pump, if the teacher will let you. And they always peek through the cracks in the outhouse door. My brother doesn't go, he helps my father, so I walk by myself and it takes a long time but I'm never late. Sometimes in winter my father drives me in the sleigh, just the two of us wrapped up warm, and sometimes if there's too much snow I don't go at all and my mother and I make a cake, with the little ones getting in the way. All the lines in my mother's face go down, but not when she helps me with my lessons after supper. Then her eyes glow black in the lamplight and she reads from my books, her finger under the words, and if my father's there, she says, *I didn't know this, did you know this?* She's not so good at arithmetic but she loves to memorize poetry, and sometimes we chant together all around the kitchen because you have to stand up when you say a poem. My mother says school is the most important thing, and she never keeps me home, not even on wash day.

———

My father says there are no jobs for one-legged men, so he looks after my brother while my mother cleans people's houses. When she comes home she lies on the couch with her feet in his lap, and he rubs them for ten minutes before she starts supper. My father can fix almost anything, and people bring by old toasters and radios. My mother says he should put a sign in the window, an ad in the newspaper, and he says maybe he will. Then there would be more money. At night when I'm going to sleep I hear the sewing machine whir; my mother has to make new dresses for school because I'm growing so fast, or she cuts up one of her own that she doesn't wear so much. I long for a blue dress like Jane at school, that she bought in Bowen's downtown.

When I was little, Black Star *was* a horse, but now that I'm older I have to pretend. We still have lots of adventures. Sometimes I'm an Indian brave riding bareback and sometimes a cowboy with a lariat and a special place for my gun. Sometimes I'm a boy or girl from long ago, riding my horse to school every day. Black Star gallops down the gravel road and along the bumpy path by the river, her mane flying in the wind, brushing my face as I bend low over her neck. I can't bring her with me when I go to visit my father because there's too much traffic, and anyway there's no river to ride to. Only a playground with swings and a slide, and monkey bars that I can go across twice. Usually when I visit my father we go to the movies, or stay home and watch TV with a big bowl of popcorn. In his apartment you can hear people walking overhead and sometimes loud voices late at night, and that reminds me.

———

My mother says, *Don't go down to the river,* but I go every chance I get. Which is not so often; there's always something to be done, or watching the little ones. Once there were twin babies who died, and when my mother cries in the kitchen, I think it's because of them. When she cries in the kitchen she always stops when I come in and wipes her eyes on her apron. I say I'll make supper although I don't really know how, and she hugs me so tight I can't breathe, but I don't mind.

I have another secret place in the barn, high up in the hay. But it's scratchy and dust gets in your throat. That's where Lady goes to have her kittens; she's always having kittens. My father says if she has any more he'll have to drown them, but he doesn't mean it. He strokes them sometimes and they let him and when he's milking they twine around his feet and he always fills up a pan for them and they all drink together, all the different colors of them. Once there was a gray kitten floating dead in the horse trough. It was strange to think of it falling in with a splash that no one heard.

My mother stays up late at night sewing clothes for me to wear to school because I'm growing so fast. In the morning she puts on her cleaning dress and her comfortable shoes that are starting to come apart at the soles. When she comes home she kicks them off at the back door, but later she sets them neatly side by side. At night she puts cream on her hands and special gloves, but they're still red and sore-looking. When she strokes my forehead before I fall asleep, I feel the smooth skin of the glove, not her hand.

I'm growing so fast I'm too big for things already; too big to sit in my mother's lap, although my brother's not. Too big for the Tooth Fairy, too big for my bike, but I ride it anyway, my knees bumping the handlebars. If my father fixes lots of radios he might buy me a new bike for my birthday, and I know the one I want. It's red and gleaming in the window of the hardware store, and every time I go by I check to make sure it's still there. For Christmas my mother gave me a diary, and I keep it under my pillow. She promised she'd never read it, not even when she changes the sheets. In my diary I wrote, *I never ever want to grow up and get old.*

After school I don't go home, I go to Maggie's next door until my mother gets back from work. Maggie has a baby named Arthur and a little boy named Stephen who's only in kindergarten so there's not much for me to do there. I watch TV with Stephen or sometimes I do my homework because that always makes my mother happy.

My mother works in an office that gives her a headache. When my mother has a headache, she has to lie in her room with the curtains closed and the lights off until it's better. She wears a big T-shirt with a picture of Mickey Mouse, one my father left behind. I make my own supper; I only know how to make grilled cheese sandwiches, so that's what I have, and I'm always careful with the stove. After supper if my mother doesn't have a headache we play cards, or sometimes we sit on the porch rocking in our rocking chairs while she drinks a cup of coffee. She says I'm the best daughter in the world, and I know she's the best mother.

On Saturdays after we do the shopping and clean the house, my mother lies down with her book and I take Black Star for a ride. Usually I go down by the river, even though I'm not supposed to. It's not at all dangerous down by the river, but my mother doesn't know that. There's a big tree with branches that sweep the ground and make a private cave. I have a collection of stones hidden there.

If I jump, I can reach the lowest branch and pull myself up, and then I can climb the rest like a ladder. The branches ooze with sticky sap, and I like the smell on my hands. If I climb high enough I can see the whole river snaking away, the roofs of houses among the trees. I can see the roof of my own house, and it's strange to think of my mother lying in there while I'm spying from far away.

I have friends at school but I only see them there, or sometimes in town when we all go to the fair. It's wonderful at the fair, all the people in their best clothes and the torches when it gets dark, all the fair smells. My mother wants to win a ribbon with her pies and preserves, but Mrs. Anderson down the road always beats her. For days before the fair, pies sit cooling on our kitchen table, surrounding the jug of flowers my mother keeps there. My mother loves flowers, and when she's walking by, she might put down whatever she's carrying, bend her head and smell them. Then her face looks like it does when she recites poetry, all soft and far away.

Sometimes there are other kids down by the river and we play hide-and-seek, or red rover if there's a lot of us. Then the river is just like the schoolyard or the vacant lot. We climb trees sometimes, seeing who can go the highest. It's usually Bobby Makin, his red shirt only a flicker way above our heads. I don't climb trees; I get dizzy when I'm off the ground, but nobody teases me about it anymore. I still like it best when I'm all alone there. I can bring my diary because the river's a good place for writing things down.

In the winter there's never anyone at the river, but I only go when the snow is not too deep. Once I built a snow fort with high walls and a pile of snowballs for ammunition. I was late for lunch and my mother was angry, but my brother fell down and cried so I didn't have to tell her where I'd been. My snow fort stayed for weeks, just the edges getting smoother. If I had matches, I could light a campfire and send smoke signals to someone on the other side of the river. On the other side there are trees, like here, but they look different. Sometimes I imagine there's another girl over there, just like me, my twin. If you had a twin you would never be lonely, there would always be someone who knows how it is to think your thoughts. Usually in winter the river still runs in the middle, dark water, but sometimes it's all frozen and then I could walk across and find that other girl.

Sometimes when we ride down to the river Black Star goes left instead of right, and we follow the path to where the big kids sit on the riverbank, lighting matches and smoking cigarettes. I'm allowed to use matches to light the candles when we have a special supper, and I'm always careful, I never throw them away with smoke still rising, like the big kids do. It's always noisy with the water going over the dam. The big kids talk and talk, but I can only hear some words. They never seem to notice us watching. Sometimes they throw one another in and sometimes they walk along the edge of the dam, where the water rushes over. Once a girl had a plastic jar and a wand and they blew bubbles until it was empty. Sunlight making them all kinds of colors, up to the branches of trees. One burst on my nose, but they still didn't notice and I thought maybe we were invisible. It would be good to be invisible at school sometimes, when no one wants to play with you.

At night the little ones snort and snuffle and I lie awake in the moonlight, thinking about the dreams I want to have. I hear my father get up and go downstairs, and when I go in to ask my mother she tells me the MacKenzies' barn is burning and we watch it from her bedroom window. Across the field we can see the orange glow and flames shooting high and the black shapes of horses rearing as men try to lead them to safety, and I know my father is there, doing something brave. When my mother says it's time to go back to bed, I say *Carry me,* and she does and I try to pretend that my feet don't knock below her knees, try to pretend that I'm small enough to be safe in her arms.

The next day after lunch the little ones go to sleep, and I go through the fallow field and down the path to the river. The flowers on the kitchen table are losing their petals, and I am picking new ones to make my mother smile. To make my mother smile I am picking the biggest bunch I can carry. Down by the water's edge there are some yellow ones growing, but I have to be careful; the riverbank is slippery and the water runs cold and deep.

My father is in his workroom, trying to fix a vacuum cleaner. My mother reads to my brother; it's a story about mice and she reads parts in a high, squeaky voice. I put on my leggings and boots, my coat and hat and mittens. The icicles on our front porch drip in the sun. It's hard going through the snow to the river, but I like the way there are only my tracks to be seen. I could be an explorer heading for the South Pole. The trees are dazzling in the sun, and there is no running water in the middle of the river. I break branches off a big stick and use it to test my way. This is the day, I think, that I will finally get to the other side.

After supper we play cards or sit on the porch in our rocking chairs, but tonight my mother has a headache and she tells me I can take

Black Star for a ride, as long as I'm home before it starts to get dark. At the bottom of the hill Black Star turns left instead of right, but none of the big kids are there, it's just me alone with the sound of the water rushing over the dam. I sit down where they usually sit and think about things I've heard them saying. Then I take off my shoes and socks. The top of the dam is slimy beneath my feet and the water is cold, pushing hard at my ankles. I think that I don't have to go right across, only a little way. I'm afraid to do even that, but my mother says that sometimes in this life you have to do things you're afraid of. I think she'd be proud of me, though I can never tell her.

I stay here all the time now; I can never go home again. Sometimes sunlight splashes on the water and sometimes there's snow and ice. Day becomes night, becomes day again, wheeling by as fast as the clouds in the sky. Sometimes I think how it all would have been different if I hadn't gone down to the river.

IN THE STORY
THAT WON'T BE
WRITTEN

In the story that won't be written there's a girl called Alice Grant. That is the name I have given her; I no longer remember her real name. It's a cold night in January 1914, and stars blaze in the sky. Alice Grant walks through a sleeping town toward the frozen river, her skates bumping against her left knee.

I first saw Alice Grant in a photograph when I was visiting my friend Laurie. This was while my daughter was staying for a week with my husband and his new wife. Every night Laurie and I sat at the kitchen table, drinking wine and talking with the dimmer switch turned down low. Her husband read magazines in another room; before he went to bed he always came to the doorway to say good night. I wondered if they talked about me.

On my last day Laurie canceled her afternoon appointments and took me to an old house that had been turned into a museum and tearoom. We drank our tea on a large, shady veranda; there were plates of cookies and tiny cakes. The house sat on a hill looking over the town. It wasn't much of a museum, a few rooms with old furniture, newspaper cuttings and photographs on the walls. In one room there was a photograph of the graduating class of the local academy, taken in 1912. About twenty students, mostly girls, although four or five boys with slicked-down hair stand near the back. In the very back row are the teachers. A tall man with large eyes and a center part; you know most of the girls would have had crushes on him. A young woman with a high, frilled collar, a tightly buttoned jacket with sleeves puffed at the shoulders. An older woman in black or dark brown, with round spectacles and a large brooch. She would be in charge, stern but fair. All of the girls have long hair pulled back, some with large bows sticking out. They wear striped or white blouses, dark skirts that reach to just above the ankle, button boots.

Alice Grant stands third from the right in the front row; beside her is a girl who must be her friend. They are the only two wearing coats, long jackets that reach to the knee, and you realize that it must be early spring, the others all shivering in their vanity. Alice Grant is the only one wearing a dark top, round-necked, and you wonder if she is in mourning or just indifferent to fashion. Where the others have trim belts at their waists, she wears some kind of jumper, the bib visible through the open buttons of her coat. The sleeves of the coat brush the knuckles of her hands, which are clenched at her sides. Her hair is dark, swept back from her forehead. Her chin is up, her expression serious; she looks ready to take on the world. A caption beneath the photograph mentions that Alice Grant later married the man who owned the house we are standing in. Looking at her photograph, I wouldn't have guessed that this was her future.

In the story that won't be written the girl who stands beside Alice

Grant is called Addie and has been her friend since childhood. The two of them causing much head shaking in the town, always going their own way. In the photograph Addie also wears a long jacket, though hers has a velvet collar. Beneath it she seems to be wearing a shirt and a man's tie. The coat has bulging patch pockets; maybe they are filled with scraps of paper, bits of string, or maybe they bulge from the way she shoves her hands in, striding through the town. In the story Addie has gone to New York to study medicine. She writes Alice letters telling her to come down there, to find herself a job, go to art school, anything. The day before she left, they climbed the rough ladder to the old tree house, sat on the narrow platform with the wind rustling their skirts.

My daughter is now almost fourteen. She wears her hair cut savagely short; I used to brush and braid it, as my mother did for me. My daughter wears lace-up boots and baggy pants and T-shirts. The other girls her age, the ones I see walking around in groups, all wear bell-bottoms and short buttoned tops. Sometimes in a clothing store I pull these things from a rack and my daughter curls her lip. When I was her age I had three best friends. We wore oxford-cloth shirts with button-down collars and did everything together. One summer we did nothing but play canasta and make fudge. My daughter's friends have all fallen away. She comes home from school and goes straight to her room, and soon I hear the music snarling. When she was younger we used to sing along to my old Mamas and Papas album. California dreaming. Dedicated to the one I love.

After I left Laurie, I couldn't stop thinking about that photograph. I finally called her and somehow she got me a copy of it, and it's been sitting on my desk ever since. In the story that won't be written Alice Grant sits down in the snow at the river's edge and takes off her thick mittens. Her cold fingers fumble with the skate laces; she takes one lurching step, then another, and soon she is gliding easily. There is a high, cold moon. She thinks that no one in the world could imagine what she is doing at that very moment.

My daughter used to skate for hours on a rink in our backyard. Her friends came over; they played crack-the-whip, and their laughter rang out in the winter air. My husband went out with the hose on the coldest nights, coming to bed late with icy fingers and toes.

I've been staring at the photograph of Alice Grant for years now, and I know some things about her. I know that she is making a decision, out there on the dark, frozen river. Perhaps about a proposal of marriage, or perhaps that decision has already been taken. It may be the night before her wedding, she may have spent the day looping pine boughs around the banister, around the archway into the front room. She may be trying to imagine herself walking down the stairs in her blue silk dress while Mrs. Stimson plays the piano. She may be trying to picture Jack; she may panic because she can see only pieces of him. The set of his shoulders, his flat, round ears, one green eye. She may be thinking of the private life of families, of passing her parents in the hall in their dressing gowns, of her mother's hair hanging down at the breakfast table. The things they talk about, the little jokes. She may be thinking that when she takes Jack's arm she will be stepping away from all of that, that it will never be the same again.

When the leaves change color my daughter and I go out walking. She comes grudgingly but she does come, scuffling along in her clunky boots. I point things out as we walk. The house we used to live in, the swing still hanging from the maple tree. The school she used to go to, the corner where she fell off her bike and needed stitches in her forehead. I tell her that at the time those years seemed to go on forever, that it's only now I realize how quickly they've passed. My daughter says nothing.

I have a friend who says she never talked to her children when they were babies. She says it never occurred to her, and anyway she would have felt silly. I talked to my daughter from before she was born, and she herself started talking before she was a year old. My husband used to call her his little chatterbox. There was a time when I believed I knew every thought that went on in her head.

In the story that won't be written there are a lot of details to be checked. Would Alice Grant have boot skates or strap-on blades? Was the weather in January cold enough to freeze the river? What color would a wedding dress be? I tell myself these things matter and spend far too much time in the public library, going through almanacs and old magazines, books of photographs. Often the other tables are filled with high school students working on projects. Sometimes after supper I ask my daughter if she wants to watch TV with me. "Homework," she usually says, and disappears up the stairs to her room. Whatever she's doing in there, it's not homework. Her teacher called me in and said that her grades are slipping, that she hands in assignments late or not at all. That she's not working up to her potential. "He hates me," my daughter says while we're doing the dishes. I tell her that from now on she has to do her homework at the kitchen table, where I can see. That her teacher will send home a list of assignments. "I'm not a child," she says, and slams the door.

———

Alice Grant trips on a bump in the ice and falls, striking both knees hard, bringing tears to her eyes. She kneels and cries on the cold, dark river beneath the ghostly overhanging trees. Thinking, *It doesn't hurt that much.* She has already written to Addie, saying, *I know what you think but it won't be like that, my marriage will be a great adventure.* Jack's parents have bought them a little redbrick house, only four years old, and her own parents have bought most of the furnishings. The sofas and chairs are already in place, just waiting for them to step through the door. They will have children, three or four, maybe, and in a few years Jack will take over the running of the mill. They will move to a bigger house and maybe there, she thinks, maybe in the big house there'll be a room just for her. She tells herself that it is wrong to think that way, that she is starting a new, shared life, that this is what she wants. She remembers Jack's hands about her waist. She remembers the games she and Addie used to play, being famous painters or arctic explorers. She remembers that when they were children she was the bold one, stepping out onto the fallen tree while Addie shouted warnings from the riverbank.

Lately my daughter has been refusing to visit her father. The Weasel calls and says that my husband is upset, that they miss seeing her, that she's so good with the children. I promise to talk to her, but all she says is "They're always calling each other *honey,* they're always kissing, it's disgusting." I can't think of anything to say to that.

In the story that won't be written there's an open door. The significance of the date will not have escaped you. Even so. If I hadn't seen the caption below the photograph, the story would have been written long ago. But I did see the caption, and I feel some obligation to the past. The problem is the photograph, propped against my desk lamp. Alice Grant looks straight at the camera, her chin tilted up; she just won't fit into the world I have made for her, the future I know to be hers.

Beside the photograph of Alice Grant is another one in a wooden frame. My daughter, two years old, at a summer cottage we used to rent. There was a game she liked to play there, with a low orange chair that we set on the beach. She would fling herself backward into the chair, her feet flying up, her laughter wild, over and over again. The photograph is taken at just that moment. There is sand, there is blue sky visible through the orange webbing of the chair. Sunlight shines on her long blond hair. Her feet are flung up, but you can still see her face, you can still see that she is laughing.

THE MANUAL OF REMOTE SENSING

The first thing she fell in love with was his name. "Gabriel," he said, holding out a hand at a party. And she has wondered since how different it might have been if he had held out a hand and said "Chuck" or "Steve." Perhaps not so different; the second thing she noticed was his hand. Long squared fingers, supple, and a jagged scar snaking across the first two knuckles.

She is walking down a winter street when the words begin. Past shopwindows draped with tinsel, skiffs of artificial snow. Heavy bags pull at her arms and a tin of something bumps against her left leg and she remembers Woody Allen in some movie. Slumped on a couch with light sparking from those glasses, speaking to a tape recorder: idea for a short story. Click.

Gabriel had different stories for that scar, depending on his mood, his audience. A fight in an alley or a wound from a jealous woman, some small, touching act of heroism. He had different stories for everything, but she didn't know that the night she fell in love. The night he told her, among other things, about the scar, the geese, the farm.

"My mother was having an operation," he said.

She'd been preparing him for days, but he hadn't paid attention. When the man in the green truck came, he clung to her legs, crying, *Why why why.*

"They had to pry me loose," he said.

They pried him loose and his mother cried and the man carried him outside and placed him on the front seat of the green truck, locked the door. Fluffs of gray wool clenched in his fingers. The man smelled and the truck smelled and the farmhouse was big and cold. Except for the kitchen, where the woodstove burned. Where the woman with red hands lifted lids and stirred things and spoke to him in a ragged voice through clouds of steam.

In the mornings they ate oatmeal, silently, while the early light crept into the room. Swelling the space, revealing the battered armchairs and piles of newspaper, the flat pallets of eggs, flecked with dirt and wisps of feathers. Touching the rusty tools and the bits of string lying forgotten in corners. He had a special spoon, rounder than the rest, and a bowl with a brown glazed design of a village. Trees and houses, a wandering stream. He stared at the bottom of the bowl until the woman told him it was time to go outside. Helped him pull on the heavy red sweater that was slowly taking on the smell of the truck, the man, the house. She spoke to him kindly and sometimes rested a rough hand on the top of his head, but he never told her about the geese, never thought to tell her.

"You know how it is," he said. "When you're a child."

She could see it all when he told the story. How he lingered near the back door, scratching the hard ground with a pointed stick, saying, *Please please please, don't let them see me.* She sees it all—the bare black trees, the stubbled fields, a curdled November sky. The red sweater, thick wool matted from washing, and his hair much lighter, hanging forward over his deep blue eyes as he feigns great interest in the tangled patterns he scratches in the hard earth by the back steps. His body tensed, clenched tight against the first faint cry, the sound that means he's been spotted. Day after day they find him, chase him if he tries to run, circle him in until he can only climb slowly, backward, perch on the top step while they hiss around him, teasing with their beaks. Until one day he hits out with the pointed stick, brings it down wildly on a musty brown back, and in an instant its mate leaps—mate or mother, depending on his audience—snaps at the stick hand, rakes his tiny knuckles, raising a long thick curl of blood.

And she sees him running and crying, running and crying down the rutted lane, past the falling-down barn. Bright flashes of red beneath a huge November sky.

She wonders about the geese, stamping her feet at a red light while a number of gray cars slide silently by. She can't trace the geese, but the farm is familiar; she went a little mad there one long windy spring. Walking the fields with a large black dog, the sound of crows. She remembers lying awake in a cold upstairs room, saying, *Hold on, hold on.* Chanting through the long, long night.

⎯

That particular version was a seduction story, and he told it very well. The motherless child, the strangeness and the fear. The way he tried to laugh about it but didn't quite succeed. The way he lowered his head over a coffee cup at her kitchen table, looking up through thick lashes. Now she sees it all as a story, punishes herself by remembering the way her fingers trembled, reaching out to touch his hand. Now she imagines what she could not possibly have seen; a slight smile on his lips as she bends over his tender wound.

The apartment is dark and quiet, but she knows immediately that Martin has been there. A trace of a scent, a sense of things not quite as they were. He's left a mug and spoon in the sink, a folded newspaper on the table. The classified section with an ad circled in red: *GUILLOTINE OPERATORS. Steady employment, some shift work. Experience preferred.*

I thought you would laugh, he will say if she mentions it. *No hard feelings.*

"Gabriel," he said, holding out his hand at a party, and they drank warm beer from bottles while the music thumped around them. Later they went out for a breath of air and kept on walking, all through the night. Their shoulders bumping, walking beneath ghostly trees, their fingers clasped, finally, as they walked past the shadowed verandas of the old brick houses in the center of town. Their sandals rasped on tiny stones and they spoke to each other straight from the heart, or so it seemed.

A mean wind blows in about midnight, throwing snow and making the windows rattle. They are old and heavy, set in wooden frames;

no sound gets through from the outside. Only the rattle in the wind, a ticking clock in the dark.

The first night without Martin she stretched and stretched, touching every corner of the bed. The second night she dreamed, terribly. Woke distant and heavy-eyed, turning up the radio to cover the hollow sound of her footsteps on the wooden floor. The smooth voice of the announcer, telling the death of thousands, in earthquakes and volcanoes, in clouds of poison gas. Hijackers throwing severed limbs onto an airport runway, followed by the sound of a man with an artificial heart eating breakfast.

And she almost called him then, said, *I was wrong, never mind, I made a mistake.* Said, *I don't mind if you fall in love once in a while, so long as you stay with me.* She almost called, but instead she made coffee, rearranged the books on the shelves. Bought a braided rug for the hollow floor. The dreams have stopped, but there is still a mean wind rattling the windows. The sound of a clock in the dark.

At work she spends over an hour with a young couple going to Greece for their honeymoon. They wear identical earrings, small gold crosses, and want to know all the options. Her fingers tap the keyboard, checking prices via London, via Amsterdam and Frankfurt. She watches through the window as they cross the snowy parking lot, holding hands, until a green Jeep pulls up and obscures her view.

Sometimes he called her six times a day, sent flowers to the store where she worked and once a telegram that said *Quit your job. Stop. I miss you all day. Stop.* He bought presents, wrapping her in long fringed shawls, the works of certain poets, and she stifled the small, mean voice that said it was usually with her money.

"How are you," he said, "you look tired, relax, put your feet up." Massaging her temples with long, cool fingers. Making dinner, opening her cupboard doors, throwing together this and that the way a Swedish cook had showed him on a fishing trawler, or a café owner on some back street in Naples. She thought she would never get to the end of him.

"But I thought your father was dead," she said, and he gave her a look full of patience, said, "Sometimes you are so literal. What I meant was . . ."

It was a long hot summer, and she was in danger of losing her job through being so often late or inattentive, and she didn't care at all.

But sometimes she didn't see him for days, a week; the telephone ringing in an empty room, curtains open to the dark when she walked past his house late at night. Once she knocked anyway and he appeared, tousled, talked to her soothingly in the hallway but said no, she couldn't come inside.

"I told you," he said later, "right from the start." And he had, that first night, walking through the scented streets.

"I seem to have bad luck," he had said, "with women.

"I'm selfish," he had said, "and totally undependable.

"I'm bad news," he had said, tracing the line of her cheek with the tip of a finger.

In the dentist's office she keeps her eyes closed, listening to a conversation from the next room.

"But what does she want?" the dentist says. "I'm afraid I don't understand—what's the matter with it?"

A woman's voice goes on and on in a language she doesn't quite recognize, and then another woman speaks in heavy English.

"She says that the tooth you have made is too small. Also that it is not white, it is not a white tooth."

"But it matches her other teeth—see? Show her, doesn't she see how it matches?"

"Yes, yes, I know, but she doesn't want it. She wants a bigger tooth, yes? And very white."

Being in the office reminds her of Martin; the reason they decided to get married, or so they told their friends. He had a job with a dental plan, she kept losing fillings. She remembers that they made a fire in the evening and lay at each end of the couch with their feet meeting in the middle. Some law of physics, perhaps, the way their feet braced together just so, not pushing one way or the other.

"Listen to this," Martin said, turning the pages of a book he was reading. "Just listen to this. There was a woman having nightmares, reliving a traumatic experience. They found a lesion on the memory point, they found a scar, and they zapped it with lasers or something, and the memory disappeared. Just think of it."

She concentrates instead on the names of the instruments. Matrix, explorer, burnisher. Quiet requests and the soft *tic* of metal on metal. The assistant sits on a stool on the other side of the chair, and her uniform whispers as she reaches for the explorer, the burnisher. The drill whines, but there is no pain. Once she opened her eyes during the ceremony and saw their two faces very close to her own. Intent, peering deeply into her mouth as if the rest of her did not exist at all.

—

"Is this what you want," Gabriel said, his hands on her shoulders, his face over hers. "What do you want, is this what you want is this what you want."

The freezing comes out slowly, replaced by a gentle ache. She sits at her desk, tapping a hollow rhythm with a pencil, writing things down and scratching them out. Wanders the apartment, restless, turning pages, touching the telephone. And finds herself standing on a chair in the closet. Shifting cartons and bags and file folders, a lost running shoe. Pulling down a white shoe box, dusty, with dented corners, feeling a new pain coming on as she takes out different objects, maps and coins and matchboxes and crumbling cubes of sugar in faded paper wrappers. Pulling things out until she finds the core of the pain, a photograph, slightly out of focus. She and Hart looking at each other in front of a tiny house in Germany.

He set the timer on the camera and balanced it on a snowbank, and just as she was looking at him and saying, "It will never work," and just as he was looking at her and saying, "Trust me, just trust me"—just then they heard the click, and while she looked into the lens, astonished and too late, he slapped the back of her neck with a handful of wet snow, saying, "I told you, what did I tell you." She pushed him as hard as she could and he fell, or pretended to fall, and they chased each other and touched cold lips and noses. They were very young, although they didn't know it.

It started in Munich; in the lobby of the youth hostel a group of laughing Americans swept her up, saying, "You look hungry, you look tired, come and have dinner with us, we know this great place." And Hart was the quiet one, smiling shyly and saying, "Why don't you come. If you want."

She'd just stepped off the Magic Bus and nothing seemed quite real. Rattling up through Greece and the flat center of Yugoslavia in a haze of smoke with Pink Floyd playing loud, day and night. Pausing only at gas stations where all the men were short and square and wore loose black suits, white shirts, narrow dark ties. She tried to explain the strangeness of this over dinner, but the food and the beer and the warmth of the room made her voice sound far away, and she stopped talking, let it all float by her.

The Americans were working in a town farther south, running ski lifts and washing dishes, changing sheets. They'd been saying good-bye to a friend at the airport, a boy named David who had already passed into legend. "Good old David," they said, "do you remember the time . . ." Someone said, "Where are you headed?" and someone else said, "Why don't you come and spend Christmas with us?" and they all said, "Well, even if you don't ski, it will be a great party, and the town is perfect, just like a postcard, you really should see it." "Maybe," she said. Maybe, meaning no. And the one called Hart sat smiling across the table with his foot resting softly against hers.

After dinner they were all going dancing, and in the cold street Hart wrapped his red scarf around her neck and said, "Sleep well." Walking backward away from her, he called, "There's a train every day at four. If you change your mind." And she saw the shape of the words coming in clouds from his lips.

In the morning the Americans were gone and she walked through the city, checking routes and the prices of tickets. Friends were waiting in London and she had plans, a place to stay, the promise of work. But her mind kept slipping back to a warm dream, possibility. The shape of words rising in the night. On the train she told herself that it was just talk, after all, and she planned how she would walk through the empty station and find a cheap room somewhere close, look at the mountains in the morning and be gone by noon, and no one would ever know. But then the train slowed and she saw him standing on the platform, shoulders hunched and dark head bare to the cold; she saw him standing like that and wondered how she ever could have doubted.

Hart came from some small place in Virginia. "Where?" she said. "Where?" because she loved the sound of him saying it, and she loved it when he said her own name, drawing out the vowels and wrapping them around and around her. They stayed in a run-down cabin that belonged to someone he'd met, two rooms with stone floors and faded carpets and a long low window so they could lie in bed with a pile of blankets and the tiny electric heater glowing red, watching the snow fall. The color of Greece faded slowly while they learned each other, where they had been and how close they had come to meeting in a dozen cities all over Europe. They told the scars on their bodies and all their small hurts and fears, and with her eyes closed she could find, easily, that place on his back that made his whole body twitch.

And the town really was like a postcard, ringed with high mountains and filled with bright houses painted with flowers and colored patterns, the main street piled high with snow that had always just fallen. That was one part of the town, the painted houses and the clean snow and the small cafés serving tea in tall glasses.

But there was also a McDonald's with discreet golden arches; there were groups of American soldiers on holiday, bright ski jackets and pink crescents of skin glowing above their ears. Four hotels named for famous generals and a PX that sold six different brands of peanut butter. "How *American,*" she said when Hart walked her up and down the aisles, past pyramids of ketchup, past Twinkies and boxes of cornflakes, Wheaties. But as she said it, she saw that she'd gone too far. "What does that mean?" Hart said, as if he didn't understand at all, and he walked fast out the door and she had to hurry after him, grab at his arm, say, "I only meant—"

And that was when she knew that she was living inside out, nerve centers all on the surface, and a word, a tone, even a certain look could make her feel such pain.

They walked and walked, still angry, past cafés and ski shops, past the butcher shop where Christmas geese hung by their cracked feet. They walked and walked and in the end, because it was late, they went into a tiny place to eat and when the bill came they didn't have enough money and they hissed and blamed each other and finally Hart told her to wait, drink coffee, while he made the long walk back to the cabin. Watching him leave she knew with a sick certainty that he wouldn't come back, that he would leave her there, bluffing, lingering over a cold cup of coffee while the owner wiped all the tables, flipped over the chairs and the sign on the door, and sat down behind the till, chewing on a match and glaring while she pretended to be lost in thought. But just when she had decided she would have to confess, to offer her silver earrings, her five-dollar watch—just then Hart walked through the door and they left with the lights flicking out behind them, door slammed and bolted.

On the way home she made him laugh, describing her ordeal, and by the time they opened their own door things were all right again. Later they tried to remember what the argument was about, and said that they couldn't.

Christmas came, and there was a party at the General Addams with kegs of beer and loud music, dancing, and she whirled around the floor with her hair spinning out all around, overflowing with love for the world. She was kissing a soldier in a doorway when Hart walked by, looked and kept on walking, hard, and she had to chase him again, pulling on her coat as she went and feeling the sudden cold outside, and the silence. They were the only things moving in the mountain-ringed streets, and he didn't stop but he did slow down. "Come on, Hart," she said, "come *on,* it's Christmas, that's all." Not even trying to explain about the soldier, all the soldiers, and how they looked in their clean jeans and their red Christmas sweaters, pink scalp showing through their close-shaved hair. The snow squeaked and their breath rose in angry clouds and finally Hart said he was sorry, that he couldn't believe what it felt like when he saw her there, that he could have killed someone. And that was the night they put a name to things and called it love, began to say it to each other. All the next week Hart stayed home from work, and they went for long walks and took pictures with his camera, sitting on snowbanks or in the old wooden armchair; they paid a fortune to have the film developed right away and pinned the photographs all around the room. On New Year's they stayed in bed and drank a bottle of wine or maybe two, and every so often one of them shuffled to the kitchen, wrapped in blankets, came back with a plate of cheese, crackers, and they ate them under the covers. At midnight she was standing in the tiny kitchen, drinking a glass of water with the stone floor freezing her feet, and the moon was reflected in the sink full of cold soaking water, the curved side of a saucepan, and she heard the church clock strike, heard sudden whoops and the blast of shotguns. When she got back into bed, Hart warmed her feet with his cupped hands, and she thought that she was perfectly happy.

New Year's Day they woke late, moving carefully. Hart went out walking, and she washed the dishes and shook the cracker crumbs out of the sheets, swept the floor. It was snowing again, and the light was gray and a little eerie, coming through the long window. Objects softened, yet distinct, and she was very aware of her body, sitting in the chair by the window, the scrubbed wooden surface of the table, a crumpled pack of Winstons, red and white, and the rasp of the match as she struck it. Through the window there was an enormous gray sky, snow piled everywhere and falling down in large soft flakes, and she sat in the chair until Hart appeared, filling up the space, snow settling on his shoulders, hair, while they looked at each other through the window. He'd found a shop open somewhere, bought bread and meat and cheese, thick slabs of chocolate, and they ate it all slowly, savoring each taste, and it was only later, when they'd closed the curtains and turned on the light, it was only then that Hart said, "There's something I have to tell you." Part of her had always known it, but it was the same part that had told her he wouldn't come back to the restaurant, told her he wouldn't meet the train. And he had done both those things.

Hart began to speak in his soft Virginia voice, and he told her that he'd been thinking a lot about home lately, about a girl he knew there. "You mean Denise?" she said, and he said, "Yes. Denise." Drawing out the vowels, lingering over the soft *s*. He told her that he'd been thinking about himself and how he was living, day to day, no plan; he told her that he'd gone out walking and he'd gone to the *Bahnhof* and he'd called Denise and they'd both cried, or almost cried, and she'd said would he please come home. And he'd said maybe, said he was thinking about it. "But you told me about Denise," she said, "you *told* me," and he said that he couldn't bear it, that he hated himself for hurting her this way. "Then this is all a lie," she said, and he said, "No, don't think that, of course not. But it's not real life either, is it?"

She took a train to London, and all through the long journey she watched for him, expected, against all reason, that he would be waiting at each station. Even in London she waited, working in different places through a winter that was raw and wet and lonely, a spring that was much the same. For a time she typed letters in a Japanese bank; the men were small and gracious, forever offering cups of tea. Hands stretched out toward her, tiny silver spoons in saucers. When she remembers that time she sees cold rain falling, hears the delicate rattle of fine china.

And Hart went back to Virginia, and he married Denise and he went to law school and he called her once, years later, said, "I'm drunk. How are you?"

She and Martin were giving a party and she could barely hear. She stretched the cord as far as she could, around the corner, but the line buzzed and crackled, and she could hear his voice but couldn't make out the words. She tried plugging her ear with one finger, shouting down the black holes of the past, saying, "What, what did you say?" Saying, "Hart, I can't hear you, call back, call tomorrow." "I will," he said, but he never did.

There's a clock ticking somewhere, beyond a pool of light. She's sitting on the floor with a white shoe box in her lap, wiping at her eyes with an old red bandana and thinking that it was all so long ago. Although his name wasn't Hart. And she's never been to Germany.

PEACH

‒‒

I'm thinking about peaches, thinking about the way things get done. This is the day after a funeral. I'm thinking about my own fingers, sticky with juice, slicing peaches into a bowl and wondering if that was why the knife slipped, why I baked three drops of my blood into a pie. It has rained all night and the trees are dripping, sodden mounds of leaves in all the bruised shades of peaches cover the grass, the sidewalks, and roads. There is music playing, viola; it circles around and around but never seems to arrive at the center, the point.

I learn some facts about peaches by opening the old encyclopedia, releasing the smell of someone else's house on a rainy afternoon. I read that the peach probably came from China, like fireworks and pasta, that Spanish explorers brought it to the New World, that for centuries its cultivation was confined to the gardens of the nobility. On the same page I read that the African peacock (*Afropavo congen-*

sis) was discovered in 1936, after a search that began in 1913 with the finding of a single feather.

But about the peach, I read that it develops from a single ovary that ripens into a fleshy, juicy exterior and a hard interior called the stone or pit. I read that peach trees are intolerant of severe cold but require some winter chilling to induce them to burst into growth after a dormant period. Also that most varieties produce more fruit than can be fully developed; some shedding of fruitlets takes place naturally, but the number remaining may have to be further reduced.

I'm thinking about peaches because I baked a peach pie on the day of Maisie's funeral. Thinking about peaches so I don't have to think about Maisie, who lived long enough to sit slumped in a chair in a hallway, long enough for everyone to think she'd already been dead for years. Thinking about the burnished skin of peaches, glistening with droplets of water in a blue bowl. Thinking about the texture of the flesh and the sudden stone at the heart, looking like something you would never expect. You would expect the smooth seeds of the orange, the delicate pips of apple or pear. But not the gnarled pit of the peach, full of rough, hidden places, so hard to work free.

Thinking about peaches takes me back to a hospital room, one I thought I'd finished with years ago. Outside that dark window, autumn rain fell through the flickering streetlights, steady and cold. Inside, where we were, the radiator gurgled and your breathing machine hissed and thumped. *I'm here,* I whispered, but nothing changed. I slid my palm beneath yours on the sheet, and my body remembered how it used to feel, reaching up to take your hand, and the way we walked with the sun going down over the lake, pine needles and sand soft beneath our feet. And of all the times we had done that, there seemed to be one particular time I yearned toward. I thought of a little house in a cave of trees, of the light glowing behind the windows, a door opening. As if it were the heart of some mystery, the center of something I needed to understand, or at least remember.

In the hospital the sheet was rough, your hand a dry, frail thing, and I wondered where you had gone.

In those days there were still trains, and that was how Grace first came there. The train ran along the edge of the lake, and the afternoon sun reflected so brightly that she had to close her eyes. Once her eyes were closed, the rhythm of the train took over, and the rhythm of the train said *help-me help-me help-me.* She opened her eyes, astonished, and made herself look at the other passengers. An old man with luxuriant eyebrows, a woman in a mauve dress with several young children, two older women with small brown hats. All people going home from somewhere, she was sure. Sure that she was the only one traveling to a completely new place.

She had come because of Maisie's letter, mostly, but there were other reasons. Because she had struck a child, because her father had burned his tongue on the soup. She often thought of that, years later. Looking through a rain-streaked window, something bubbling on the stove behind her. Her father waited until she sat down, unfolded his heavy napkin, picked up the gleaming spoon and dipped it into the bowl with a *chink,* grimaced and made a *tch* sound as it touched his lips, his tongue. That was all, but in that sound she heard everything. That it was all her fault, that she had made the soup, brought it to the table too hot, failed to warn him. That he would not complain, that he was tolerant and reasonable, that she did her best but it was not good enough.

That alone wouldn't have done it without Maisie's letter lying on her bedside table. Without the incident with the boy. No one would blame her for hitting him, and in theory she wouldn't have blamed herself. She'd been warned about him, a troublemaker from the start. A shifty-eyed child in mismatched clothes, always muttering and whistling under his breath, always picking at the sores around his mouth and nose. There was a strange flash of satisfaction in his pale eyes as her hand came down; she noted that with some cool part of her brain but didn't remember it until later. For what really shook her, as her hand met flesh, was the thrill of white-hot fury, the way she could have gone on and on, the struggle to make herself stop. Sitting back at her desk with the boy sniveling in his seat, having the others stand and read, one by one, her nails digging into her palms until she could dismiss them and flee to the cloakroom. She was not a fool; she understood that her life was not as it seemed.

The train made its way along the lake to the tiny redbrick station. Pausing on the dim step, she saw the blaze of light that was the outside world, saw her own right foot in its laced shoe, the toe pointing down in the act of stepping out, already warmed by that light while the rest of her stayed in shadow. *This will be something,* she thought as her other foot met the ground, raising a small puff of yellow dust.

Please come, Maisie's letter had said. *There'll be all those old women telling me how to take care of a baby, but I'll need some real company.* So she knew about the baby but she was not prepared for how Maisie

looked, her face rounder and her dark hair curling around her forehead and cheeks in the heat, the way she seemed to be so full of life,
bursting with it. They had known each other at the Education Col-
lege, talked and laughed in Maisie's small room where she hoarded
crumbs of food from her infrequent visits home. The boardinghouse was clean but cramped, the other boarders set in their ways.
Still, Grace couldn't help envying the life as she hurried home
through darkening streets, blowing her breath before her, her mind
already preparing her father's dinner.

So they studied together and fretted together and walked giddily
down rain-soaked streets. They thought they would be friends forever, but Grace stayed in the city and Maisie went back to teach in
the country school near the place where she was born. Then she
wrote to say she was marrying a boy she'd known all her life; their
wedding trip brought them to the city for a day or two, but Grace
and her father had gone for their annual visit to the cousins in De-
troit. Maisie had to give up the school after the wedding, but she
was busy all day on the farm, and she wrote letters about all the
things she was pickling and preserving, in a way to make Grace
laugh.

The young man standing beside Maisie in the summer sun had hair
the color of polished wood and wore a soft blue shirt with the
sleeves rolled up to the elbow.

"You must be Jim," Grace said, holding out her hand, startled by
Maisie's whoop of laughter as his fingers met hers.

"No no no," Maisie said, "Jim's haying. This is Harry. He wants
to show off his new car, so I said he could drive us out."

Grace wondered later if she'd had some inkling in that first moment of the new way her life would go. Things seemed charged and strangely clear, but she thought that was just the daze of the journey, the bright sunlight falling all around them. They climbed into the car and drove through the town, which was gone before she had time to even notice it. A wide, dusty main street, a few drowsing horses hitched to wagons, a small boy pulling at a sitting dog on the end of a rope.

"My father had the first car in town," Harry said. "Before the war. But it was nothing like this beauty."

She noticed how his voice drew out the word *beauty.* Then they were climbing the hill at the edge of town, sunlight slashing at the lake in the distance, and out in the open country where the sound of their traveling made conversation impossible. Harry's hands were square and easy on the steering wheel, although his eyes were narrow with concentration.

"I promised Jim I'd drive slow with Maisie along," he shouted. "But later I'll take you for a spin and show you what she can really do."

Grace just smiled, holding her hair down with both hands.

Grace soon learned that Harry was a terrible tease, and she herself the kind of person who made it easy for him. That first day he told her all the things he'd found in the stomachs of fish caught in the lake. A diamond ring, a baby's rattle, a set of keys, a soggy prayer book. At the prayer book Grace realized she'd made a proper fool of herself, saying *Goodness* and *How could that be;* she was grateful that he didn't seem to hold it against her. In the sunlight on the front porch he handed her a peach from a basket near his feet, and it seemed he was offering her much more.

Maisie's Jim, when he finally appeared, was a bit of a surprise. Looking so much like one of those fresh-faced country boys she had described, the ones she was so glad to be away from in the city. Red hair slicked down and all those freckles, even on the backs of his hands. He had hands that would look clumsy, hanging down from a jacket sleeve, holding a pen or pencil. Resting briefly on top of Maisie's head as he passed by. He didn't talk much, but you could tell how he felt about things just by looking at him looking at Maisie.

Later that night, after Harry had gone and Jim had climbed the creaking back stairs, they sat up talking in the kitchen, and it was like the old days in the boardinghouse on Cobb Street. Except that Maisie was greedy for details and Grace could supply them. What women were wearing in the city, what shops had closed, what new places had opened. Maisie was like a person cramming for an examination, like someone galloping to the end of a good book, eager to start on the next. Grace wondered again why she hadn't stayed, why she had come back to the place she was so eager to get away from, but she couldn't ask. Not sitting in the solid farmhouse kitchen, not looking at Maisie's thickened fingers, resting on her huge belly. Once, pushing herself up from the chair, she paused, her knuckles white on the table, and said, "Oh, Grace, how'd I get myself into this." But then she laughed and Grace thought she'd been joking. She'd already seen the chest of baby clothes, each stitch tiny and immaculate, although Maisie claimed to be useless at such things.

It was very hot those first two weeks, the countryside shimmering, filled with the sound of clicking insects. Harry came several times to take Grace driving, along dusty twisting roads, over rackety bridges where they could look down and see small boys wading in the sluggish river. Sometimes they stopped at a tiny store or a farmhouse and drank something cold before going on, and Grace told him things that surprised her, things that were true and yet not true. Like about Arthur being killed in France—it was true that she wrote him every week, true that she packed up tin boxes filled with jam and candy and warm woolen socks. It was not true that he'd meant any more to her than all the other boys she went to school with, but that was the part she didn't say. True she helped her father with his research, although usually that just meant transcribing his scribbled notes. With Harry she felt like someone who fit the facts of her life, someone she could perhaps become.

Going around with Harry she learned that he knew everyone, not only by name but by history. As they drove away he would tell her strange, scandalous things about the old man who'd poured them a glass of lemonade, the woman waving from the farmyard gate.

"That can't be true," Grace would say, laughing and holding her hair.

"I swear," Harry said, turning his head to look her straight in the eye.

There were moments like that, when Harry looked right at her, that everything else disappeared. But she told herself that was nonsense, that he only took her about because Maisie asked him to. One night after Harry had been to supper, Maisie said he should take Grace to the party he was going on to. A little house in the little town where everyone knew him and slapped him on the back, knew who Grace was too and smiled at her. The house was overflowing, rugs rolled back and people stomping on the floor in time to the fiddles played by three old men sitting on kitchen chairs. The two of them sat on the grass just outside, Harry resting on his elbows with his legs stretched out in front, feet crossed at the ankles and moving in time to the music. Grace thought she had never seen someone so completely at home in the world. On the tail of that thought, Harry spoke out of the dark.

"Do you ever think," he said, "that things are just too easy?"

"No," Grace said, "no, I never have found that."

It was very late when Harry drove her home, the car like a cocoon moving through the dark countryside, and she thought that he might kiss her then, and he did.

Maisie was waiting up in the darkened kitchen; she had trouble sleeping these last days. Grace didn't see her at first, just heard her voice coming harshly out of the dark.

"Well, you have the look of a girl in love," Maisie said, but Grace just laughed.

They sat up talking, as they usually did, and most of their talk was about Harry. He didn't say much about himself, but Maisie seemed to know every detail, and Grace thought it strange that she had never talked about him in the city. That night Maisie told her about Harry's mother, how she'd walked into the river behind their house, leaving him a baby sleeping in a buggy. His father found him out on the riverbank when he came home for lunch. It was the talk of the town, but no one could find an explanation. All the books, perhaps. And then the way his father married again, but a child does need a mother, after all.

Grace almost wept, sitting there at the kitchen table; she could see it all so vividly. The baby who was Harry, cooing and waving his arms about. The woman in something long and white walking smoothly backward, her eyes on her child until the last possible moment. It gave Harry an added dimension, this story, as if he carried within himself the dappled riverbank, the sound of willow leaves in the wind, the rushing water. She thought this even after she saw a photograph of Harry's mother, hanging on a wall. Large and heavy-featured, she looked like a woman waiting to roll up her sleeves and get on with something. A woman who, having made up her mind, would stride into the cold water without a backward glance.

Maisie wanted them all to have a picnic at the lake, but it was too close to her time to go driving so far in a car or wagon. So they set up a table outside the house, packed everything in a big hamper and unloaded it on a flowered cloth. The table was under an ash tree, bright red berries clustering, and Maisie sat on a kitchen chair with her back to the house so she could pretend it was a real picnic.

"It *is* a real picnic," Harry said, and to prove it he produced two bottles of last year's cider, and they all drank it and got quite giddy. Jim started to laugh at something Harry had said; he laughed with a helpless, whooping giggle that got them all going, holding on to their aching sides. Grace thought of the rain-colored rooms of her father's house, thought, *This is where I belong, right here with these wonderful people.*

Jim went to check something in the barn and the three of them stayed around the table, talking about nothing in particular. A fellow Maisie and Harry knew who was in the veterans' hospital, how his wife still took the train to see him every week, five years later. Grace knew that Harry had just missed the war, had been on his

way in England when the bells rang. He hadn't said, but she sup‑
posed he would feel guilty about that, about feeling relieved about
that. And Maisie talked about her plan to have Grace stay. She
said the young fellow who'd taken over her school wasn't working
out, that she was sure the trustees would hire Grace in a minute.
They could find her a house in town, she knew exactly the place.

"Harry'd like that, wouldn't you, Harry," she said, and her voice
was loud, although she was smiling like always.

For some reason not clear to any of them, Maisie decided she
wanted to taste a red berry. She climbed onto her chair, then onto
the table, planting her feet apart on the flowered cloth, reaching up.
That's dangerous, Grace thought, but lazily, for Maisie was laughing
as she picked a cluster of berries, laughing and saying, "What do I
do now? How do I get down from here?" Harry was laughing too;
he got to his feet, opened his arms wide, and said, "Jump—I'll catch
you."

There was a moment when Maisie could have stopped herself;
Grace, watching, saw that moment come and go. Then a long, slow
moment when her huge shape hung in the air, before it collided
with Harry, before they both went crashing to the ground. Maisie
came up still laughing, pushing herself until she was half sitting,
and cuffed him hard across the head, saying, "Aren't I the great
ninny, then, thinking you really could."

The next night the baby was born dead, and Harry asked Grace to
marry him. She thought about that later, how it hadn't seemed
strange at all. Thought about poor Jim with his freckled hands
hanging heavy and useless, and Maisie pale and weak in the upstairs
bedroom, the terrible sobbing that went on and on until finally she
slept.

Harry was sitting on the porch steps, smoking a cigarette and looking into the night. Grace sat down beside him and he put his arm around her; she rested her head on his shoulder, too tired to care what he thought. The lights from the house fell golden on the grass in front of them, beyond that only the mysterious shapes of trees, brooding and rustling.

"Would you ever think of marrying a fool like me," Harry said, and she said, "I would. Yes, I would."

Harry was a joker and a tease, and his wit was often cutting. Cut Grace. When she first knew him he forgave her for that, but later he became impatient. "Oh, I was only joking," he'd say, "can't you take a joke, Grace?" And then he'd get angry and the lightness would be spoiled, and it would be all her fault. He taught their children that, that she couldn't take a joke, and she knew no matter how many times they'd seen her laugh, that would be part of the picture they had of her. Part of the role she played, like hosting teas and baking things for sales and carefully choosing new hats for church. She was astonished to realize, in her later years, that this was her life. She'd thought it was something she was moving toward, the same way she'd thought she was moving toward Harry. She'd thought she would someday come to understand the contradiction that he was, all that teasing and then his black days, days when he wouldn't speak a word, when he'd sit in a darkened room or in the car in the driveway and not answer whoever came to call him for supper.

He came back after his black days, he always did, and she allowed it. She thought perhaps that was why he had chosen her, why he had seemed so sure. That he recognized some darkness in her, or some respect for darkness that would permit things someone like Maisie would only snort at in her gruff and sunny way.

——

In the beginning they saw a lot of each other, the four of them hav-ing meals together or an evening of cards, going to the fall fair. Then, in the fifth year of their marriage, Jim fell from a high place in the barn, and everyone wondered what he'd been doing up there. Maisie thought he'd been after a kitten that had gotten itself stuck. "He's such a softie," she said, "that would be just like him."

Jim had probably been dead for hours when Maisie found him, had gone looking when he didn't come in for dinner. The kitten, if there had been a kitten, was long gone.

At the funeral Maisie was very calm, although hours before, she'd been sobbing in Grace's arms in the cold kitchen. Raving about how Jim didn't deserve it, how she was a terrible woman. Grace reminded her how much Jim had loved her, how plain it was to see, but that didn't help, and in the end she could only smooth her hair until the crying stopped. She supposed it was something to do with the baby; she knew they'd had some trouble over that. Jim wanting them to have more and Maisie holding back.

Jim's brothers took over the farm, as was only fair. Maisie walked away, leaving almost everything behind—the big double bed, the pictures on the wall, the curtains in the windows. They paid her enough money to buy a house in town, the same little house she'd thought of for Grace that first summer. People talked about the bare windows, but Maisie just shrugged and said, "I've got no se-crets to hide." Said, "If they don't like what they see, they shouldn't be looking in."

Grace knew her stubbornness and so, while her own babies were sleeping, she stitched and stitched until she'd made brightly col-ored curtains for every room of the house. One wild fall day she piled them into the buggy and wheeled them over, the blue air filled with spiraling colored leaves. The house was set back from the road and looked quite nice; Harry had been helping to paint and hammer things into place. It was planted with pine trees all around, not maples and elms like the farm, but they were still quite small, and Grace felt like a giant striding to an enchanted cottage. They hung the curtains and then drank tea, cupping their hands to warm them in the kitchen with its table and two chairs. Until the children started to whine and she took them home, pausing to look back and feeling quite pleased at the way everything was decently covered, and Maisie waving cheerfully from the front door.

Harry's father was dead and his stepmother had moved away and he lived still in the square stone house and that was where he brought Grace, after they were married. He didn't mind what she did, so she set about changing every room, painting and papering and buying furniture. Their four children were born one right after the other, and she found that whole months could pass without her having what she would have called a serious thought. She was blissfully happy.

It was during that time that Maisie fell apart for a while. Telephoning late at night, in a state, and Harry would put on his trousers and go to her. Well of course Grace couldn't walk through the sleeping town, leaving her little ones.

"She was *drunk*," he said the first time he came back.

Maisie had taken a job in the school outside of town, walking the two miles there and back in all kinds of weather. Often she was late, and the children would race inside to sit at their desks when they saw her appear on the crest of the last hill. Through the windows they watched her stop at the pump in the yard and duck her whole head under. There was talk, but people made allowances.

Grace's father had been heavily sarcastic about the life she was going to. He referred to Harry as "your young farmer," although he knew very well that he was a lawyer, like his own father, and an educated man. He feigned astonishment when Grace told him they would live in a large stone house, not a cabin made from rough-hewn logs. She told herself that he was covering the fact that he would miss her, but she had an uneasy suspicion that he might, in fact, be exactly what he seemed, a terrible snob.

He came to stay with them each Christmas, complaining about the journey and about the drafts in the house, although Grace knew well that it was warmer than his own. She thought that he might soften, holding his grandchildren on his knee, but he took little notice of them unless they behaved badly and he could criticize their upbringing.

During the rest of the year she telephoned every Sunday evening, until once he didn't answer and she knew that it was as she imagined—his cold body lying somewhere in the big dark house while the telephone rang and rang. She called the neighbors, paced her downstairs rooms until they called back, their voices tight with the drama of it all. She was surprised that she didn't grieve more, all those years they'd spent together. She did find, though, that she thought more about her mother than she had in years. Grace was eight when her mother died, and when she thought of that time, she remembered her paddling away in a canoe, over a calm lake with the sun going down. This was not likely to ever have happened; her mother was not athletic, and where would they have kept a canoe? Still, the image was so clear that Grace had always accepted it as part of her string of memories. It was only when she thought about it that it became strange, like someone else's memory, or a dream.

She didn't tell her children about that when they came to an age of wanting stories of her life. There was little enough to interest them, she thought, so she told them stories from Maisie's life instead. "Tell us," they would say, with the covers pulled up to their chins, "tell us about the time there was a blizzard and Maisie had to sleep in the school all night. And they ran out of wood and had to burn all their notebooks so they didn't freeze into ice blocks. Tell us about the time the goose chased Maisie away from the outhouse, the time she drove the big wagon and the horses ran away. Tell us about the time Maisie put stuff on her hair and it turned bright orange and she had to wear a scarf for weeks. Tell us a Maisie story."

After a few months Maisie wasn't late for school anymore, although there were still days when she slept with her head on the desk while the older children helped the younger ones with their sums or listened to them read aloud. She stopped calling in the night, which was just as well, because Harry was out most evenings at some meeting or other, coming home late, tired and not talking. But she also stopped dropping by; they hardly ever saw each other, and when she had time to think of it, Grace missed the giddy days of their friendship. She invited Maisie to teas, to Sunday dinner, an evening of bridge, but she usually begged off at the last minute. A headache, a toothache, a pile of examinations to mark.

Grace thought it was probably her fault, thought she'd grown boring, surrounded by her babies. Some days she thought it was hard for Maisie, seeing her with her family, and some days she thought the fading away was part of growing up, of having a mature life. It was ridiculous, really, how long it took her to work it out. Her youngest child was starting high school; they were coming out of church one blue Sunday morning, Grace caught a little behind. Maisie stumbled on the bottom step, and in the way Harry reached out to steady her, Grace suddenly saw it all. In the unthinking, automatic way he took her arm, then let it go, without even having to look at her, to say a word. It hit Grace like a fist to the stomach, and she felt such a fool.

That particular Sunday they had invited Maisie for lunch. Grace took to her bed and heard them all downstairs laughing and talking. Maisie tiptoed upstairs later to see how she was feeling, and the bed creaked when she sat on it. Grace's jaw clenched so tight she could barely hiss, "Get out of here."

"I thought you knew," Maisie said that night on the telephone. "Oh, Grace, I thought you always knew."

Grace set the telephone down, hard.

She stayed in her bed for a week with a terrible, aching fatigue, rearranging everything she knew about her life. Her youngest daughter carried bowls of soup up the stairs, smoothed her hair from her forehead, and Grace wept to think someone would be so kind to her. Harry sat on the side of the bed, holding her hand and saying it was all over, saying he was sorry, and she turned her face away. She felt a fool for all the years of trying to learn Harry, for feeling they could arrive at some place together, when she'd been hobbled all along without even knowing. Everything was shaky now, and she wondered about those days long ago. She remembered that hot summer, Harry holding out a peach, and what happened with their eyes when she met his gaze; now she wished she could push the frame out and see the look on Maisie's face. She thought about that first day, the puff of yellow dust rising around her leather shoe, and she thought she could get on a train again, ride it into another new life, but she knew she wouldn't. She thought about those nights sitting up in the kitchen, Maisie's hands clasped on her swollen belly, talking about Harry, and she groaned and turned her face into the pillow.

But what do you do when your heart is breaking? In the end you just go on. Grace rose from her bed after a week with a feeling that something had hardened inside her, something that would never be soft again. She thought she wouldn't speak to Maisie for the rest of her life, but that wasn't how it worked out. The town was small; they were always running into each other at the butcher's, in the drugstore, on a sunny corner. The part of Grace that cared had turned to stone, and she found it wasn't so hard to say a few words and then walk on. Not even hard to face Harry across the supper table, to watch his hair turn gray. To go with him on winter trips to Florida, to stroll on the beach with her arm in his, to watch their children marry one by one. Years went by, ten years, twenty, and it was only sometimes that she thought of the smooth sheen of a peach in Harry's brown hand and knew that it could have been another way.

When Annie's baby died, they brought their other granddaughter to stay for the summer, and Grace thought how good it was to have a child living in the house again. One night she made a special supper of all the girl's favorite things; Harry was having one of his black days and didn't eat with them. The child sat at the table with a coloring book while Grace washed the dishes, and when she was wringing out the cloth she caught sight of herself in the curved side of the big corn pot. Without thinking any more about it she called the child to come for a walk, and they moved through the long shadows of the town, through summer air scented with flowers, until they came to the place where light glowed behind Maisie's windows in the little house set back from the road. They walked through a grove of evergreens, grown so tall, and knocked on the blue front door. And Maisie opened it as if she'd always known she would.

I'm thinking about peaches the day after a funeral, thinking about my grandmother and the way we used to walk when the sun was going down. Thinking about my grandfather in the dark house behind us, and how we left without a word. How once we came to a house in a cave of trees, all the night birds settling there. "My friend Maisie lives here," my grandmother said, and I remembered all those stories my mother liked to tell and missed her with a sudden pain.

The woman who opened the door was wearing an old plaid dressing gown, and her face was scrubbed and shining. "Oh Grace," was all she said. Inside, she turned on more lights and the night leaped black beyond the windows. They sat me on a couch with a game of jacks that came from a string bag, while they sat at the kitchen table, their hands wrapped around mugs of tea. They talked and talked, but I didn't understand a word they said.

After a long time they started to laugh, and then they called me into the kitchen. "You must try these peaches I've got," Maisie said, "they taste like a mouthful of summer." She turned from the sink as she spoke and light flashed from the blade of the dripping knife, from her shiny forehead and cheeks. My grandmother was wiping her eyes; she said she was happy, not sad.

Maisie reached for a plate and the knife flashed again. She set it down in front of me, resting a cool, wet hand on my head and saying, "There you go, sweetheart," as if she'd never known my name. Their voices swooped and laughed over me as I stared at the thing on the thick green plate. A peach split in half with an aching hole in the center, wriggling red lines pulsing out from that place. I was sure I would taste blood, and I did when I bit into it, and something thickened in my throat and my eyes were suddenly running with tears. My grandmother took me in her lap as if I were much smaller, and rocked me back and forth, and when the tears finally stopped I felt lighter than air. At the door Maisie pressed something into my hand, something hard and rough. "Take this," she said. "And if you plant it well, maybe something will grow."

This book was set in Bembo, a typeface based on an old-style Roman face that was used for Cardinal Bembo's tract *De Aetna* in 1495. Bembo was cut by Francisco Griffo in the early sixteenth century. The Lanston Monotype Company of Philadelphia brought the well-proportioned letterforms of Bembo to the United States in the 1930s.